THE NEW BIZARRO

PRESI

SEX DUNGEON
FOR SALE!

PATRICK WENSINK

Eraserhead Press
Portland, OR

THE NEW BIZARRO AUTHOR SERIES
An Imprint of Eraserhead Press

ERASERHEAD PRESS
205 NE BRYANT
PORTLAND, OR 97211

WWW.ERASERHEADPRESS.COM

ISBN: 1-933929-86-3

SEX DUNGEON FOR SALE! was originally published in *MONKEY-BICYCLE* and MY SON THINK'S HE'S FRENCH was originally published in *HOBART*.

Printed in the USA.

You hold in your hands now a book from the New Bizarro Author Series. Normally, Eraserhead Press publishes twelve books a year. Of those, only one or two are by new writers. The NBAS alters this dynamic, thus giving more authors of weird fiction a chance at publication.

For every book published in this series, the following will be true: This is the author's first published book, we're testing the waters to see if this author can find a readership, and whether or not you see more Eraserhead Press titles from this author is up to you.

The success of this author is in your hands. If enough copies of this book aren't sold within a year, there will be no future books from the author published by Eraserhead Press. So, if you enjoy this author's work and want to see more in print, we encourage you to help him out by writing reviews of his book, telling your friends, and giving feedback at www.bizarrocentral.com.

In any event, hope you enjoy…

—Kevin L. Donihe, Editor

For Leah

Thanks to: Mom and Dad for everything (sorry about the title). Sara Farr, Don Thrasher and James Greer for all their encouragement. Kevin and the Eraserhead crew for all their hard work.

TABLE OF CONTENTS

- Sex Dungeon for Sale!.....................................8

- My Son Thinks He's French...........................10

- Wash, Rinse, Repeat.....................................15

- Chicken Soup for the Kidnapper's Soul..........26

- Clean Bill of Health..31

- Donor 322..34

- You Can't Blow Yourself to Smithereens on an Empty Stomach..39

- Jesus Toast..42

- Pandemic Jones...49

- Me and Gerardo, Down by the Schoolyard..........69

- The Many Lives of James Brown's Capes...........73

- Johnny Appleseed's Punchateria......................84

FOREWORD

HOW DO YOU describe *Sex Dungeon for Sale!?*

Lord knows thousands of man-hours and entire governmental budgets have been gobbled up answering that very question over the years. As we now know, many people came close to solving the mystery, but ultimately failed. And, of course, most died.

If you'll allow me, I'd like to take a different approach to unraveling this literary milestone.

This collection of stories reminds me of a folk tale passed down from generations in my family. Maybe you'll agree.

Once upon a time, there was a renegade soldier in Uncle Sam's army. He fought the Nazis and his name was Lt. Bruce Willis. There was no risk too big for the scrappy old soldier: he'd surf a tank while firing on enemy soldiers and drop grenades onto opposing aircraft while hanging from his plane's wing by just his teeth. Hell, once Willis even had unprotected sex.

Willis was so fearless he refused to wear one of those metal helmets or even a flak jacket. Every man in his platoon gave Willis their utmost respect.

Well, during the Battle of the Bulge or some such fiasco, our hero was deep behind enemy lines, leading a scaredy-cat pack of soldiers on a mighty killing spree. Suddenly, a sniper rifle rang out. Willis fell to the ground while the others took cover. When the coast was clear, the soldiers turned their beloved, pig-headed lieutenant over and saw a bullet hole near his heart.

The platoon gasped with sorrow.

One of them reached into Willis' shirt pocket and pulled out a thick bible with a round hole through the middle.

The platoon gasped with hope.

With shaky fingers, that soldier opened the Good Book to see if the bullet passed through. As the pages cracked, his face turned ghostly.

"What is it?" one asked.

The soldier with the bible looked up at the crew. "It's been hollowed out."

The group gave a despaired groan.

"For whiskey?" one soldier asked.

"For a gun?" another said.

"Don't tell me there're nudie pictures of men in there," one soldier said. This guy was the prick who always got on Willis' case, saying Bruce wasn't a real American man, calling him a sissy.

"No," the bible-holding one said. He stuck his fingers in the space between the hardback covers. From that hollowed-out holy book, the soldier fished up the world's tiniest bulletproof vest, the size a doll baby would wear.

The platoon gasped in surprise; hope filled their faces.

The soldier used his other hand to pull a crumpled piece of lead from the bible's gut.

The platoon gasped with more surprise. Faces bloomed with more hope.

At that moment, Lieutenant Willis' eyes popped open and he reached for his sidearm. In an instant, Willis shot the soldier that accused him of owning naked pictures of gentlemen. The man dropped limp to the ground, a cherry pie-like mess attached to his neck.

"Lieutenant, why'd you do that?" one soldier asked.

"Open up his shirt. Our friend here is an undercover agent. A Nazi," he said before lighting a celebratory cigarette.

And sure enough, the man had a swastika tattooed on his chest.

-P. R. Wensink, Literary Scholar

SEX DUNGEON FOR SALE!

OKAY, SO THERE'S one more room to see. Careful, the stairs are a little on the steep side. Fifteen hundred square feet, washer/dryer hookups…oops, easy, just a few more steps. And, let me see, it's perfect for that home gym you were both telling me about.

Ha…folks, honestly, you're not the first to ask. How can I put this? The home's current owner uses this basement as a *rumpus* room.

No, no, speaking as a person who has seen a *lot* of real estate over the years, I think *sex dungeon* is too harsh a term.

Let me just emphasize the amazing *space* this room has to offer. It practically doubles the size of the house. Now, bear with me for a second, but can't you picture a treadmill in this corner? Or maybe a nursery? With your eyes and your hair, you two will have some gorgeous babies.

Ah…another good question. You know, I'm not a doctor. I have no way of knowing whether that's a gynecologist's table or not.

No, I wouldn't touch. It looks antique. My guess is it's some sort of European recliner…with stirrups.

Let's focus on three words here: Tons-of-Storage. Just look at all these cabinets. There's no telling what we could lock up.

Oh, um, well I don't know what that is. Yes, I suppose those are chains. Really, let's just put the padlock back where it belongs and move over here. There's so much to see. Time is of the essence. I already have three other couples scheduled to view this property today.

Oh, shoot. I should have mentioned not to wear flip-flops down here, ma'am. Okay, full disclosure time. There are some issues with puddles, as you can clearly see.

I'm sorry. Puddles of what, you asked?

I'd call that rumpus. But honestly, for the price the owner is asking, this is a minor problem. I've seen homes with dirt basements that sold for twice this price. Folks, this place is a steal.

Another excellent question, sir. Most people don't notice the walls. Boy, you two have really done your homework.

I wish I knew all this when I was looking for my first home.

God, me too. What did we all do before the Internet?

Yes, the walls are unique, aren't they? That's soundproof paneling. I'm told it's the highest quality on the market. You can really see the craftsmanship.

Certainly, feel free to touch. I doubt there's any rumpus on the walls.

Ma'am, didn't you mention playing the clarinet? Well, you could toot your horn at all hours and the neighbors would never hear. Isn't that fabulous?

Why does the current owner have them?

This is your first home, right? Then let me tell you a secret. We homeowners are always picking up pet projects that never come to fruition. Take my husband. He *had* to have a table saw last year. Do you think he's ever built me a deck? No. Same thing with soundproofing your rumpus room. Who knows? Probably an impulse buy, just like a *People* Magazine at the checkout counter.

Okay, so what do you say we take another look at the backyard? We're talking barbecue central.

…No…I can't say I heard anything. This is a great neighborhood for kids, probably just some tykes out playing football or tag.

Well, yes, I suppose the soundproof panels would work both ways.

Boy, you know, folks, there's an even bigger padlock on that door back there…and a sheet covering it up. I don't think the owner wants prospective buyers inside. We should respect his privacy.

Oh gosh, I'm a city-girl. I couldn't tell you what a goat sounded like if my life depended on it.

Calm down. I wouldn't classify this as a *sex dungeon*.

Unless, of course, you're in the market for one.

MY SON THINKS HE'S FRENCH

MY SON THINKS he's French.

His new accent was cute at first, but it's starting to get on my nerves. If he asks for another glass of Bordeaux, I swear I'll be in jail for child abuse.

Yesterday, I walked upstairs to make him turn down his new Jacques Brel album, and his room smelled like cigarettes. You know, those weird yellow ones without filters. As if this all wasn't bad enough, Leah and I caught him wearing a beret.

A beret.

I sure as heck didn't go to the hat store recently, and my wife didn't buy it for him. The kid's six, for God's sake. Where does a little boy get fancy headwear like that?

Le chapeau, he insists.

This is all cable television's fault.

In order to get the new ESPN, we had to beef up the subscription. Now our household receives two separate channels of Eurovision.

But still, it's *Euro*vision, not just Frenchie-vision. I've never watched. It's supposed to cover lots of other countries, right? My boy could easily pretend he's Italian or Spanish or Dutch, even.

For crying out loud, I'd buy the little guy wooden shoes until he got splinters. But no, my son thinks he's French. Sure, it's not the end of the world, but it's just so *French*. You know?

Whenever I bring this up to Leah, she shrugs it off. She always paints me into a corner, gets close to tears and snaps something like, "Well, would you rather he sing Barney tunes or Serge Gainsbourg?" She thinks it's healthy. She emailed me a study about how most kids his age have a skull full of grey pudding from too much *Baby Einstein.*

Actually, thinking back, she's fallen hook-line-and-sinker for this whole deal. In fact, last week she watered down our boy's pancakes and called them crepes. And I don't have any proof, but I'm pretty sure we never used to buy that Nutella stuff, either.

Maybe we did. I don't know. You see, due to certain circumstances, I've only recently started paying attention around our home.

But back to the problem at hand. A few nights ago, I couldn't sleep and was watching my new ESPN channel. Bored stiff with men's curling, I went into the spare room and dug through some old photo albums. After a while, I stumbled onto my wife's college scrapbook. Never gave it a thought before, but at three in the morning it beat Canadians sliding rocks across ice.

Halfway through her senior year is a little page—a shrine is more like it. There's a snapshot with a big Magic-Marker heart drawn around the face of a strange man with lipstick kisses all over. The guy is skinny, real skinny. He's wearing sunglasses indoors and drops a cool, bored expression into the lens.

Underneath, in Leah's handwriting, it says, "Pierre" with the i dotted by a heart. A little lock of black hair was braided and slid under the plastic, too. Call me crazy, but that dude looked a little like our son.

Don't worry. I didn't flip out. Though I was real close to shaking Leah awake, screaming about infidelity like a movie on one of those crummy women's channels our new cable package gets. Then I realized her senior year of college was almost a decade ago. The math doesn't work. Leah loves me. She hates goose liver pâté. Case closed.

That didn't help me get any shut-eye, though. A sweaty guilt burned in my chest, knowing I was holding our boy back. I've heard kids who learn a second language end up something like nine-times smarter. Our boy could be anything he wanted: a doctor, a diplomat, or even own a dry cleaning business.

It's really important for kids to get every educational opportunity possible, even a heaping spoonful of French culture. I totally support that sort of stuff, really. But he is only halfway through kindergarten. Little boys shouldn't be able to pronounce *existentialism*, let alone quote entire passages of Jean-Paul Sartre, you know?

How long has this French obsession really been going on? I admit I wasn't the best husband or dad for a while there. See, just before our son was born, I snagged a whopper of a promotion. Now, spending all those extra hours at the office helps keep the company afloat and bought Leah this gorgeous house. It also keeps our son's closet stocked with capri-length slacks. I consider work a necessary evil.

Yes, that's a terrible excuse. I'm a workaholic, no argument here. Leah and I even went to counseling for a while, and it seemed like it would help. But I couldn't stay away. I'm good at my job, and people depend on me. It's a wonderful feeling to be so important. It's addictive.

However, my work ethic crash-landed a few days ago. An epileptic seizure hadn't snuck up on me since before we were married. Out of the blue, one blasted through my brain at dinner after another argument about how we can't afford any more brie this month. I'd forgotten that sensation, that helpless surge of dying. Let me tell you, lying flat on your back, waiting for your heart to turn to cement, changes a man's priorities.

Luckily, I survived and vowed to be a better person. Now, it's a strict forty-hour workweek, and I've been spending so much time with my beautiful family, Leah seems kind of annoyed. Coincidentally, that's when I started to notice my son thinks he's French.

Who cares, right? This is America, and people are

free to act as they please.

I agree, but it's an everyday struggle. He's still my boy, and I still love him. I'll stick by that little rascal no matter what crazy country he pretends to be from. But this particular phase is just more of a challenge than when he wanted to cut his own hair.

In my pursuit of being a better husband, I volunteered to clean out the garage yesterday. Digging through boxes, I found a clump of Leah's pictures. Big shocker, there was old Pierre again. It was impossible to tell just how short he was in that earlier headshot. Looks like he barely reaches past Leah's waist. The guy is tiny. Behind that cigarette and five o'clock shadow, he's not so cool. A regular Napoleon. No need to be jealous, but still, I can't shake how he looks more than a touch like our little guy.

That same night, my tyke enthusiastically interrupted tuck-in time, stating his intent to grow up a socialist. I told myself, after kissing his forehead and checking the closet for *Le Boogie Man*, that was the final straw. Drastic measures were needed. Socialism? That wasn't the boy I've always loved.

But the more I think about it, who is the boy I've always loved? What did he look like as an infant? I don't remember him toddling around, learning to walk. No idea what his first words in English were. Couldn't even tell you if he prefers hotdogs or hamburgers, though I suspect frog legs edge out both.

The elephant in the room is I'm a shitty father. You know it and I know it. My slugger's childhood is sweeping past me. I decided it was time to get serious about this situation.

I didn't have a revolutionary plan. I'm still new at being father of the year. I'm supporting my son and his Franco-American ways the best I can, and picking up another Jerry Lewis DVD wasn't the answer. I decided to surprise the family with a vacation.

I bought three tickets to Paris and left work early to surprise Leah and the boy.

I pictured their priceless, stunned faces. Hoisting daddy's little buddy on my shoulders and singing whatever happy French people like to sing. Leah smooching me a big wet kiss and whipping up dinner while I watch ESPN. Father of the year didn't feel so far away.

Sadly, walking into the house this afternoon, my vacation plans belly-flopped. It's a difficult day in a man's life when he discovers his six-year-old son has man-sized genitals and pubic hair. However, the really tough part is digesting this while the dude you thought was your innocent little boy nails your wife on the couch as she moans, "Pierre," loud enough to crack a mirror.

WASH, RINSE, REPEAT

MY FAVORITE REPORT reads, "the victim was nothing but a pile of taco meat when officers arrived on scene."

Around the country, tons of similar reports flood into police departments.

The first mistake the Supra-Kleen Dishwasher Company made was advertising the complaint hotline right on the front of its latest model. Its second mistake was installing a **KILL** setting on the dial between the **POTS AND PANS** and **REGULAR** cycle.

Currently, America is sloshing through the swamp of an epidemic. This plague slipped out its ugly womb as a speck, unnoticed at first: a nurse in Newark, a teacher in Tucson. Dead in their kitchens, dishes growing crusty and moldy, something rotten hanging in the air, as the washer waited its next command. Soon, forensic experts and plumbers were combining their powers in a nationwide manhunt.

A priest in Portland. A dancer in Denver.

Each owned Supra-Kleens, brand new models.

A sheriff in Chicago. An acupuncturist in Albuquerque.

I pin down the owner of Supra-Kleen Dishwashers, Donald Dumford III, and ask for a comment. His office has a condensed gym locker smell. The furniture moans the way imitation leather does when people take a seat. A cuckoo clock on the wall knocks back and forth.

"Look, bud. Don't blame me just because a few inexperienced operators get their timecards punched." Every hand gesture and shift in his seat is twitchy. "I'm not responsible for these idiots." Dumford's skull is covered in tiny gray corkscrews of hair. The skin around his brown eyes hangs purple with bags, and his shirt is a few shades darker under his arms.

I flip open my notepad and explain just how many

idiots have been sent to the morgue. I nudge my tape recorder closer until it practically kisses his tie.

"Jesus, god," Dumford says, wiping sweat from his temples. "Thirty-eight. That's impossible. I think you'd better talk to my lawyer."

A banker in Boston, a fish monger in Fort Wayne... and tragically, a dish washer in Dallas.

I ask Supra-Kleen's attorney—a sharp, well-dressed professional who looks like she scheduled childbirth into her Blackberry—who is responsible for all the children missing a mother now, for the dogs with no owner to feed them, for the coffee mugs that go unwashed. I remind the attorney how hard coffee stains are to remove.

She won't even let me into her office. We stand in the waiting area as assistants scurry around with thick files under their arms. "My client, Supra-Kleen Dishwashers, is committed to being a leader in the industry. Our customers demand a high quality product with a **KILL** cycle." She constantly brushes hair off her shoulder and looks back at the receptionist. Maybe it's a signal for the secretary to butt in and say someone important is on the line. "If we didn't invent it, some cut-rate company like Wash-co. would have. And I think we all know what kind of flimsy dishwashers they manufacture. Frankly, people should be thanking us that our dishwashers *have* a **KILL** cycle. If someone else produced them, there'd be three times as many deaths." She leans into the microphone. "You're welcome, America. You can quote me there."

A carpenter in Kansas City. A baseball coach in Bangor.

I speak with Wash-co. CEO Daniel Bumpus, a cool, smiley fellow with a balding head. His office is modern and comfortable and smells like a hotel room. "That's preposterous. Thank you for telling me what those rats said. Wash-co. is dedicated to being the finest automated dishwashing appliance on the market," he says. Turning slightly red and less cool, he points a finger at me. "It's absurd to think that we don't kill as many people as Supra-Kleen. Tell Dumford I challenge him to a head-to-head contest. Dishwasher that kills the most people in an hour wins."

I nod, thinking about how this assignment has given me a headache and a phobia of dirty dishes.

* * *

Nail-gun kisses.

Blisters can't get that thought out of his head. All night long, her lips stenciled across his body like a nail-gun. Now at work, he can't focus on answering the phone. A hundred other men and women, just over his cubicle wall, answer similar questions, all loosening their collars from the heat. It makes him flop his skull into his hands. Blisters can't empathize with the woman screaming on the other end of his headset phone. Her husband, a patrolman from Pittsburgh, was found dead next to their dishwasher.

"No, I will not hold again, young man." Her voice is a distorted guitar through his earphones.

Nail-gun kisses, nail-gun kisses, Tommy Blisters thinks. "Ma'am, did you husband read our instruction manual thoroughly before operating the Supra-Kleen 2000?" He lifts his head from his fingers and watches a dozen red lights blink across his phone console. A dozen more angry callers.

"Well, how am I supposed to know? What does it even look like?"

"It's pretty distinct, Ma'am." The words slip from his mouth on a train rail. He's repeated them so often. "It'll be the dishwasher instruction manual with a skull and crossbones on the cover."

He zombie-walks through the rest of his shift. Phones bounce off their hooks, and a computer feeds the calls to him. "Hello. Hello? Who the hell am I speaking with?" he hears enraged customers shout into his ear all shift long. His eyes close

17

and he imagines her smell instead of solving their problems.

After he retires his headset for the night, Tommy calls the nail-gun kisser and wants to have dinner later, thinking he would settle for staple-gun kisses or even old-fashioned hammer-and-nails action. "I don't think that's the best idea, Tommy," she says.

* * *

My second favorite police report goes, "the victim's torso and head are an unrecognizable pile of flesh. Dental records are needed for identification. Dishes, however, are spotless."

I stand behind the hot lights and the director and the camera operators in a television studio. Three old white men sit around a table, gritting their teeth and growing pink as each takes a turn speaking on stage. My stomach throws a starving fit when I smell a deli tray. I haven't eaten for days, too scared to dirty a dish, maybe.

This segment of *Nightline* is almost finished, but the guests burst into an argument each time they're allowed to speak, preventing the host from signing off.

"Harvey, I don't think it's fair to blame Supra-Kleen for these terrible accidents," Carl Dumford, Supra-Kleen's rigidly handsome public relations man says to the host, his skin tomato red around his tense neck. "I mean, sooner or later everything's gonna kill you. Take that pencil you're jotting notes with. Give it a few minutes. You could be dead," he stammers, "lead poisoning. Supra-Kleen just wants to help people with their dishes. Is that so horrible?"

A window washer in Wheeling. An accountant in Akron.

"So, you're advocating murder?" the next angry man says. "We might as well have Jack Kevorkian designing microwaves. This company should be held accountable for its actions, and Donald Dumford III should be breaking rocks in a federal prison as America's worst serial killer!"

"Now, Harvey, do you see what our industry has to put

up with? Feeble minded, so-called consumer *advocates.*" Carl Dumford points a stiff finger; angry spittle leaps from his mouth. "This dishwasher has led to the deaths of forty-six people in the last two weeks." The consumer advocate smacks a fist on the table. The water glasses slosh and spill a little.

"People like this are merely panic brokers if you ask me, Harvey. This week it's deadly dishwashers; next week he'll be whipping viewers into a frenzy over the dangers of kitten whiskers. Consumers know the risks when they buy these products."

The host hasn't been able to slide a moderating word into this conversation for the last ten minutes. It doesn't show up on camera, but from my view I see a mist rising above the set and the burning lights. Angry sweat evaporating into steam.

I need answers for my article. The deadline is close, and nobody seems to be giving any concrete explanations. My job depends on it. The newspaper is counting on me. All the pressure brings back the migraine, so I remind myself what my doctor said: "Think of what makes you *happy.*"

My blood pressure lowers with visions of my daughter playing in the sandbox and thoughts of me uncovering the truth on this story.

The jittery dishwashing publicity man, defending his industry on camera, could be a great link. It doesn't hurt that his last name is Dumford, either.

A salesman in Spokane. A baker in Butte.

"We're not saying people shouldn't be able to wash their dishes," the consumer advocate says in a hoarse voice, wiping his brow. "They just shouldn't run the risk of death and dismemberment. Perhaps some education is all. Something to stop this madness."

"Harvey, this is ridiculous. If you start limiting what cycles people have on their dishwashers, the next thing you know we'll be wrapping a noose around television shows like this one. Free speech goes kablooey." Dumford laughs the way confident people do when they think they've won.

19

"We'll all be waiting on our breadline rations before you know it. Communists. We'll be a bunch of Communists if we regulate American freedoms."

"Gentlemen, we need to go to commercial break," Harvey the host pipes up in a strong tone.

After the show, I have a tiny window to catch Carl Dumford before he slips into his limo and steams off into the night. The alley is dark and full of trash bag silhouettes. He's within an arm's length when my cell phone rings to life. The man turns his confused pink face and stares at me like I'm a pickpocket.

* * *

"Tommy, you shouldn't be here," the nail-gun kisser says. "My dad will be so mad. Shouldn't you be at work, anyhow?" She peeks from behind a cracked door, opening it inch-by-inch, fighting the urge to hug him.

Outside her enormous house, the grass is a shade of fresh green paint. A man in a white uniform mows the lawn across the street.

Blisters licks his lips, nervous: "I quit."

"Tommy, my dad got you that job." Tommy watches her speak, and his heart has a car wreck. He has no idea why all the other guys at school make fun of his girlfriend. This girl is beautiful. "He'll kill you for sure if he sees us together." She bites her soft lip and closes the door a little until only one brown eye watches the daylight shine through the crack.

"Fired was more like it." He grabs the doorknob and laces his other hand into her fingers. "I was fired. I couldn't focus on work after last night."

"Tommy," she coos, swings open the door and grabs his hands. They are speckled in red calluses from batting practice. No wonder he got the nickname Tommy Blisters, she thinks. "If you don't have a job, your dad won't let you play baseball. You'll lose your scholarship. Your future." Her

20

voice rises to a dramatic peak only eighteen-year-old girls can pull off. "You don't want to end up working for your father."

The mailman walks up to the doorway and interrupts. "Hello, young lady. I'm new on this route. Is this the Dumfords?"

"Oh, yeah, that's me." She loosens her grip on Tommy's fingers.

"Golly." The thick mailman smiles. "So, these letters are for *the* Donald Dumford, the dishwasher king?"

"Yes, thank you. I'll send Daddy your love," she says, snatching a pile of letters.

"I have a plan, sweetie," Tommy whispers as the mailman whistles down the street.

The girl wishes his last name really was Blisters. Bumpus just doesn't sound right. Might as well just change her name to Wash-co if they got married. Daddy would never allow *that*. "We can't do this Tommy. We're from different worlds."

"I'll fix everything. Trust me. I talked to your uncle, Carl. I have a plan. You guys just got a new dishwasher last week, didn't you?"

* * *

A truck driver in Tuscaloosa. A veterinarian in Valparaiso.

It's almost sunrise, and I can't think of an angle for this article to save my life. My shirt is dotted with coffee stains, and my fingers are wrinkled from all night typing. What does everything mean? That stupid manual clock over my bookshelf nags at me every ticking second.

I start writing: *The dishwasher is just like American culture. It's easy and simplifies our lives, but kills us in the end.*

I hit delete on the keyboard. My index finger stings. I want to write something my daughter can be proud of when she learns to read. I want the truth.

That's stupid, I think.

Before he sped away, Carl Dumford promised me an important phone call if I spin his representatives in a positive light. Ethically, it felt dirty, but I had no choice. Frankly, I don't even have my mind made up about the washers yet, so I told him yes. I told the PR man to call and he'd get what he wanted. My old journalism ethics teachers would be sad, but they never told me it'd be like this.

God, what's worse—the fact that America demands a *KILL* cycle, or the fact that we're too dumb to avoid it? What kind of planet will be left when my little girl grows up?

My assistant phoned with the latest numbers today. A sort of wintertime quiet wound knots in my ears after she told me, "Fatalities topped the fifty mark this evening."

A tailor in Toledo, number fifty. My lungs burn asthmatic at the thought.

I'm too young to remember, but I imagine this is what the atomic arms race was like. Did anyone need a bomb that could wipe out two million people? But that was nothing compared to the new Supra-Kleen dishwasher. The cold war would have meant countless innocent victims. This, this is some sort of clean-freak mass suicide.

When was the last time I actually scrubbed a dish? When was the last time I physically washed my car? When was the last time I hand-wrote a letter, or worse an article?

It reminds me of one of the more boring police reports: "Subject found dead in kitchen. Nothing human remained."

Is that the point?

I type: *Nothing human is left. Our humanity is down the drain.* This could be the story that bails our little newspaper out of bankruptcy.

My tired eyelids start to seal shut.

I catch myself sleeping and stiffen my back. I can't remember the last thought I had.

Morning sunbeams poke through my window as the phone rings and yanks me awake.

22

* * *

The nail-gun kisser isn't so sure about this idea. Her face bends in depressing ways she thought only a calculus test could make it do. Her mind focuses briefly on the brightly striped fish cruising around Daddy's tank. She says she loves Tommy, but this might be a little too much. "We're not trapped here, you know. Couldn't we just run away like normal people?"

"Does it need to be loaded?" Tommy asks breathless, following the tiny designs in the marble countertop. "We only get one chance to kill ourselves for love. I don't want to screw it up."

"Well, I'm not an expert. But yeah, I suppose loading would help."

"You do it. I'm shaking. Look at me. I don't have the nerve." He never tensed up like this on the pitcher's mound, not even during the state baseball championship, but now his fingers won't even budge.

"Fine, I'll do it." She huffs and opens the washer, slipping in some dirty cereal bowls and spoons. "Loaded enough?"

"Where's the guy your Uncle Carl said was coming? Where is he?" They share nervous glances and peek out the window.

"Tommy, I'm not so sure about this."

"Don't you love me?"

* * *

Carl Dumford was brief, his words smeared into long strings of vowels. He called in the middle of an all-night bender. The publicity man hated himself for what his brother, Donald Dumford III, had done. He said he'd give me a big break. The break of a lifetime. "I can't believe I'm talking to you. I should phone the police. But Supra-Kleen offered me *money*. I was weak, like a little baby, so I took it and shut up. Find my niece as soon as you can. I'd say stop them, but acts of god can't hold back teenagers, you know?"

23

There was a long silence and the clinking of ice into a glass.

"Forget positive spin now," he said. "Bury that idea six feet under. Guilt is stronger than money."

I'm struggling to find the address Carl gave me. Houses in expensive neighborhoods like this don't exactly advertise their numbers.

A beaker of acid crushes in my gut. It sends heartburn racing around my chest and up my throat. I am a journalist. I have a code of ethics. I should be the one phoning the authorities. Is guilt stronger than the story of the year?

I locate the house. I don't know how I could miss it. I've seen smaller shopping malls, and it looks like Carl said it would. I stand at the back door, just where he told me to go, with my journalistic integrity funneling down the drain.

I promised not to site the public relations man as a source. Though people will have questions. Police will want answers. I'll take that chance.

* * *

"Let's just leave a note," nail-gun kisser says, hugging her man tight, crying.

"We have to do this right," Tommy says. "Be patient. Kiss me. I love you."

"This doesn't *feel* like Romeo and Juliet, Tommy." Her tears get bigger.

"Same basic idea, I think. I never read it."

The patio door opens, and a tall man with thick black glasses and a beard walks into the kitchen. He reminds the boy and girl of their history teacher. He has a tape recorder in one hand and a notepad in the other.

* * *

My guts go violent inside me. These two are just kids, not much older than my daughter. What am I doing here? I should run. I should call the cops. I should cut the electricity.

But that wouldn't help the paper.

I swallow hard and close the door behind me.

* * *

"So, you're the guy?" Tommy says very small, like his first church confession. "The guy from the paper?"

A thick cloud of silence hangs in the room as the three eyeball one another.

"Um, okay, so do you, like, ask us questions? Or should we just turn this thing on?" The fish in the tank all stop knifing through the green water behind him. Tommy reaches for the dishwasher.

"No wait." The man puts a hand in the air and breathes like a marathon just ended. "Why are you doing this?" he says. He steps close, looks down at the Supra-Kleen and takes a step back.

* * *

"For love," the pretty girl with the scar tells me. I pray my daughter will never be so naïve. I want to tell this girl to stop, but the newspaper and its plunging bottom line prevents me.

"To teach our families a lesson," the boy says, snatching the girl's hand tight.

I breathe deep, hoping the balloon in my throat will pop soon. "Isn't there an easier way?"

"What could be easier?" The boy looks puzzled.

My little newspaper is crumpling up with my journalistic integrity. Guilt is stronger than I imagined.

25

CHICKEN SOUP FOR THE KIDNAPPER'S SOUL

AN INTRODUCTION TO
Chicken Soup for the Kidnapper's Soul

Anyone who says kidnapping is easy doesn't know the first thing about strapping duct tape to an angry set of lips.

Fact is, kidnapping is exhausting.

Whether your motives are political, financial or *other*, it feels impossible to maintain that "First Kidnapping" buzz throughout your career. Remember when you originally slipped a cloth sack over your congressman's head? Remember that unforgettable swarm of butterflies in your stomach after you threw him in the back of your windowless van? I bet that feels like a fuzzy dream nowadays.

It's common to lurk through peaks and valleys while holding a victim (or *victims,* if you're ambitious!) against their will. We've all experienced days when it seems the muffled screaming and basement door scratching will never stop. We've all been so stressed that every pothole our van runs over brings us to tears. We've all wanted to pull our hair out...or worse, return our houseguest to the playground where you found one another.

But hang in there. We're kidnappers, darn it! And we're in this together.

Chicken Soup for the Kidnapper's Soul is the only book dedicated to guiding you through this adventure we call life. In the following chapters, we'll cover useful coping techniques for experienced serial-nappers and casual weekend stalkers alike.

The important thing to remember is you're not alone.

26

Come on, did you really imagine you're the first person to think of this? I suppose the Lindbergh Baby just wandered out of its crib. And I bet the Symbionese Liberation Army didn't need a little "me time" after brainwashing Patty Hearst.

I didn't think so.

No two human thefts are the same, and nobody understands this better than *Chicken Soup*. You may be surprised, but there are some common troubles and hurdles all nappers face. Sure, your ex-girlfriend won't marry you after she's been in the trunk for five hours, but that doesn't mean you can't achieve some spiritual growth in the process. *Chicken Soup* will show you how.

Chapter One stalks the most basic human function, one we all forget in the heat of the nap: *Breathing.* Studies show proper respiratory techniques help relieve stress and clarify focus...not to mention make tying a sheepshank from bungee cords a heck of a lot easier. *Chicken Soup*'s proven Five-Step Cool Down Process™ will have you out of the basement and lurking in the shadows in no time.

Chapter Two prowls a step further. Now that your head is clear from breathing, it's time to stop dragging your tail end and plan for the future. We will discuss several methods for effective confinement calendaring using Microsoft Outlook and Excel spreadsheets. Additionally, we'll help you spot possible snags in your plan before they become nightly news material. Here at *Chicken Soup for the Kidnapper's Soul,* we say an organized kidnapper is a happy kidnapper.

At this point, you can hold your ski-masked head high. You are a calm kidnapper with a well-planned detainment. Way to go, slugger! Now is the perfect opportunity for reflection.

Chapter Three spreads open the drapes and peeps into the burning question: "What kind of kidnapper am I?" It's common—even while keeping your congressman captive in a U-haul truck until he fixes those enormous potholes by your house—to question our motives. With a short personality test, you'll learn where this burning urge to hold people against their will comes from, what kidnapping style best fits you as an individual, and what it says about you personally. Hint: It has nothing to do with your astrological sign!

One of the most popular questions *Chicken Soup* receives is: "Hey, I'm comfortable with who I am as a kidnapper, but my prisoner is a real drag. What gives?" The easy answer is, "they *always* are!" But seriously folks, **Chapter Four** is here to save the day by dissecting that question at length, making this an enjoyable imprisonment for everyone. Topics include: "**Have your kidnappees work for you!**" If you're like us, you'd love to hire a maid to stop by and tidy up the compound once in a while, but they are expensive. Meanwhile, you've got a herd of preschoolers in your attic, just itching to vacuum or wash dishes and maybe even clean out the slop buckets. Well, this answer practically writes itself. Other topics include—"**Cheer up, Congressman. I just changed your water dish.**" And, "**look, if I didn't drug you at that sorority party and take you back to my cabin in the woods, someone else would have. And they wouldn't have made shortbread cookies, now would they?**"

Whew, what a whirlwind! Talk about anxiety! Inevitably, doubt calls you in the middle of the night and breathes heavy in your ear. **Chapter Five** binds and gags the whole, "Maybe this wasn't such a good idea," stage everyone goes through. Let us take a guess. Your shoulders feel like sacks of cement; you haven't slept in days, and some new wrinkles were recently spotted below your eyes, right? Tough luck. Kidnapping is a full-time job, buster. But don't panic. This happens to the best of us. Did you forget your breathing?

Frayed nerves are part of this business, and **Chapter Five** will clear your mind and maybe your conscience. Learn to deal with the fear of life imprisonment and fend off negative publicity from your *teeny tiny congressman-napping* with spirituality, lots of laughter and old-fashioned calisthenics.

Chicken Soup's final chapter, **Chapter Six**, helps you focus on the inevitable goodbye. Throughout history, it's been next-to-impossible to kidnap someone forever. Just ask the guy who kidnapped Frank Sinatra's son. And with today's technology, Amber Alerts and excellent milk carton photography, the kidnap train has to pull into the station sooner or later.

Whether you chose to discreetly return your houseguest to the steps of Congress, duct taped inside a sleeping bag, or dream of being taken forcibly by ATF agents in a hail of gunfire, it's hard to fill the gap that kidnap victims leave in their wake. It's not unlike the sadness of an empty home when a youngest child is shipped off to college. We call it Empty Basement Syndrome (EBS).

If you think you're too tough for EBS, maybe you're not a *real* kidnapper. I bet you'd make a terrific prison guard. Holding people against their will and not making an emotional connection sounds like your cup of tea.

Chapter Six is for the rest of us kidnappers. Those with a pit in our stomachs around the time we used to empty out the feces bucket. It's for those with a migraine headache after reciting our Pothole Manifesto, only to realize that nobody with a congressional vote is tied up in the corner to listen anymore. This chapter is for anybody with that confusion burning in their hearts while wondering what to do with all those empty shackles and unused basement space. These are our people—*Chicken Soup* people—and we will cruise the road to recovery together.

It's a harsh, empty world out there, and nobody knows that like a lonely kidnapper. **Chapter Six** discusses your options at length. Recovery is a dark journey, so think of *Chicken Soup* as your flashlight. The obvious solution is to immediately plan your next caper. But when a special kidnappee leaves your life, it takes more than the satisfaction of lurking around bread lines, staking out the halls of Congress and crawling under gymnasium bleachers to fill the void. Fortunately, there are several kidnapper-friendly online chat rooms and prayer groups. This chapter discusses all the groups for your special needs.

Finally, don't forget your one last chore: a trip to the mechanic. Undoubtedly, *Congressman What's-His-Name* didn't have the political pull you hoped. Needless to say, it's time to get new shocks and struts on your window-less van...those potholes aren't going anywhere.

CLEAN BILL OF HEALTH

I JUST SLIPPED the nurse a fifty for checking my blood pressure when the doctor walks in, grim as all hell.

I barely notice him, though, because I'm wondering whether I can swing another trip to Monte Carlo before the pipe bomb in my colon explodes. Most people would be thinking about crying themselves to sleep in my situation, but not this guy. I love living too much.

"It's the darndest thing, sir," he says, click-clacking his pen uncontrollably. The office's disgusting combination of cleaner smell and the doc's aftershave makes me wish I were already dead.

I set my last minute vacation to the Rivera on hold and zero in on this man's chaffed pink lips. This same doctor told me half a year ago, with his bald head leaking sweat the same way it is now, that I had six months to live. So, when faced with the agony of recovering all by myself—no wife, no family, few friends—I decided to light the fuse on life's cannon and launch into a non-stop New Year's bash. See, I have cancer.

But I can look back on these months with pride because I didn't just whoop it up. I also gave back. Even though the world took my parents when I was six and my wife just after we were married, I'm not bitter. Would a bitter guy buy shoes for two hundred orphans?

"It's the darndest thing, really and truly…" The doctor chuckles the way uncomfortable people do when they can't bear to spread bad news. He walks from his computer screen to my chart at the other side of the room, clicking his pen the whole time. "…you don't have cancer."

My mouth is dry and my ears are suddenly ringing. My skin is itchy. I want to sprint for the door. "Well, that's interesting."

Since the day I learned about my deadly disease,

I've smashed my fist into the face of conventional wisdom. I stole its virginity and left it with an itchy crotch. Immediately after that fateful doctor's appointment, I cashed out all my savings and stuffed that fat wad into my pocket. My wealth came with an attitude adjustment and a special tattoo to keep myself on task.

Before learning about my colon cancer, I was timid and scared of my shadow. I saved every penny, but for what? I never had any fun, and that was no way to live.

During my walk toward the light at the end of the tunnel, living never felt so alive. Blood pumped through my body like I was reborn. New cars, expensive homes, vacations, personal trainers for my cat, filet of endangered animal for dinner—you get the picture. Man, living's been a blast. When I'm not writing checks to those barefoot orphans and taking them to the zoo, I'm a Scud Missile of fun.

The doctor makes a weak smile.

"Huh, wha?" I say, humming a U2 song I heard this morning.

Keeping Bono on retainer was the best investment I've made since my death sentence. It makes me wish I'd lived my entire life just to be happy. Bono sounded a little flat on the phone today. Probably because it was who-knows-what-hour in Tokyo. But I still told him he sounded great, because I know that he likes hearing that stuff.

The doctor repeats the "good" news.

I'm scheduled to die next Wednesday. I circled it on my calendar and made sure I didn't have any blind dates (talk about a bad first impression). Wednesday marks six months to the day I was told my body had six months of life left in the tank. Wednesday is, coincidentally, also when my bank account will be found floating facedown in a shallow pool. The only proof I ever existed, beyond some happy orphans, will be a massive credit card bill with nobody to pay it.

The sweaty doctor says, "We've been suspicious,

32

especially since you've been actually getting healthier and packing on the pounds." He sinks a finger into my soft gut.

"Bald Eagle steaks will do that to a man."

The doctor doesn't look convinced and keeps talking.

I remember when he first diagnosed me. He recommended chemo, which I suppose would have caught the fact I wasn't dying a lot sooner. But that sure sounds like a hell of a lot less fun.

"Oh, that's..." How do you fake being excited about a clean bill of health? "That's nice." My gold teeth give a smile, and I admire the tattoo on my arm: *Born to Die...in Six Months.*

He clicks his pen. We stare silently. Suddenly, I'm the sweaty one.

This should be the happiest moment of my life. A second chance is a man's opportunity to do all the things he never got to during the first forty-five years.

But I already did all those things over the last six months.

"Are you sure, doc?" I count faded green tiles on the floor. Now I'm broke and homeless, but I have a sack of amazing memories. But are memories enough? Is that all life ends up being?

"Turns out you only had a colon *blockage.*" He stops clicking and slaps me on the shoulder in congratulations. "Yes, you see, it was a paperwork snafu. It's the darndest thing."

DONOR 322

TO: windycity15@yahoo.com
FROM: Valgal@hotmail.com

Steve,

I know people like your friend Omar. They think they are so much better than us, just because they have a mom and a DAD. We do have a father. Donor 322. But that's cool, because now I have a family. Thank God for our website. It's soooooo awesome that we live in a time when computers bring us together. I was just recently talking to one of our sisters, Kaitlin. She lives in Chicago too!!!! But I haven't heard from her in about three months. Guess she doesn't want a little sister bothering her all the time. But she can't run from it. We're flesh and bone. Just like you and me.

Is it cool if I call you big brother????? My mom is never home, and I'd feel safer with a big brother. She works at night. She's out the door as soon as I get home from school. Sometimes I wonder why she had me. I hope your mom isn't so shitty.

I can't wait to meet you next week. I feel all warm and fuzzy about finally having a family.

Talk to you soon,

Your new little sis, Valerie

* * *

God, Valerie, you have all the innocence a thirteen-year-old is supposed to. All the stupidity of a teenager. All the embarrassingly obvious pockmarks of a future failure.

Christ, I'm falling apart as I type this. My fingertips are melting into bloodstains across the keyboard.

And, yes, I knew Kaitlin, just like I know you. Just like I knew fourteen other gray children around the Chicago area. Somehow, your mom moved to Oregon. It was a lot harder to meet you that way. But now my flight is booked. Round-trip. Chicago to Portland. One day only.

Valerie, just like Kaitlin, just like Ben, just like Patrick, just like Diane—you're paralyzed at the stump. Mushy and muddy in the head, you just don't know it. I get stomach cramps of guilt thinking about how you have nothing but a future fizzling-out with temp jobs, no insurance and flu symptoms that cling for a year and a half waiting for you. I don't want you to fail like me.

Here I am, stuck in limbo, staring at a computer monitor, writing to no one. Vomit surges across my body in waves. It butterflies into my mouth, dragging a tail behind that tastes like white deodorant. I can barely keep going, Valerie. But for you, I will.

I'm hovering over this shitstorm with a bird's-eye view, and you're the last one I need to meet.

You are correct; the Internet is nice. There was already an online group of lonely, latchkey kids in Chicago. So many years ago, their moms wanted a fleck of life from the gold bar, so they peeled it off genetically. Artificially. They wanted to connect to this ugly world the way a husband couldn't. They spent thousands of dollars back in the 90s to have a spurt of some stranger up their tubes.

Kaitlin was tough. She was a stack of bricks. A little pudge with a tight shock of black hair, already gray at the

35

roots. She sounded like a side of beef when she hit the tile floor of her mom's apartment. We wrestled like brother and sister for dozens of minutes.

* * *

TO: Valgal@hotmail.com
FROM: windycity15@yahoo.com

Your mom don't know a thing, right? I told mine I was going to Urbana for a soccer camp with my boy, Omar. She's clueless. Sounds a lot like your unit, always working and giving me cold kisses on the forehead. I have to swat her away like a bug, saying MOM, I'M NOT A KID ANYMORE. She's cool, though. Never grounds me, even when she caught me smoking cigarettes with Omar. Do you smoke? I can hook you up with a carton if you want.

I get into town at 8:30. I'll just take the bus to your house. I got your directions. It sounds real easy. I hope our moms don't get pissed. I just feel so lonely. An only child with no dad, just like you.

I get real angry, right in my chest, and it makes my head hurt sometimes. I never told nobody this, but I got suspended once for beatin up on this kid for makin fun of me. Tellin me I was a test tube baby. How stupid, huh?

Oh well, he he he;) I can't wait to meet you. It feels cool already knowing I have a sis, some blood, looking out for me.

We're meeting in front of your apartment building, right? How will I know who you are?

Steve

* * *

It was so obvious it hurt.

Just like when I lost my job for the third time in a year. Just like when the bronchitis came back. Just like when that cute girl I met at the bar stole my wallet.

There's a website for everything now: People oil painting dachshunds. Old men collecting Nazi paraphernalia. Why not a chat room for sperm donor children in the Greater Chicago area?

My eyeballs sizzle from staying up all night, typing your name a thousand times. Like ladybugs, these black and red spots kick around a fishbowl of my eyes, clinking their shells against the glass of my cornea. Falling apart hurts so much, Valerie. Thank God you won't have to deal with this.

I first hit the jackpot at the library. My electricity was shut off again, so I was forced to use their free Internet. Information slips out of computers now like a wet baby. Giant lumps of info bounce into your lap. Finding my donor number was a snap. I did have to pay fifteen dollars, but it was worth it. Even though that's all I had left in my checking.

But bang, there it was, an entire chat room support group around Donor 322. A family. They planned a picnic in the summer. Lonely kids looking for a whiff of normalcy.

* * *

TO: windycity15@yahoo.com
From: valgal@hotmail.com

It'll be easy. I'm the only 13-year-old girl you'll ever meet with gray hair!

Val ;)

* * *

I remember that day. Cold and hungry, twenty-something. Dying. A total black hole. They paid forty-five dollars to fill a tiny cup. Thirteen years ago that sounded like a dream come true. I remember thinking if someone paid me forty-five bucks each time I jerked off since grade school, I'd have been a millionaire.

I got the same look from the nurse that all women gave me. Kind of a head duck and a squint, as if to say, "Your face looks young, but your hair is so old."

I went gray at ten. As far as I can tell, so have all my kids. I'd like to think that's the only trait they picked up from their old man, but I know it's not true. My pop was a flea bag. His old man was a bum. And my great-grandpa was probably a sleaze. Being a loser runs in our blood, kids.

I feel my body evaporating. I feel my bones slither out my toenails the way water cooks out of a pot of rice. After you, Valerie, I'll be a ghost. Totally gone. No trace of me on Earth.

All my kids have to look forward to is a lifetime of upset-stomach tragedy and bad news. Nobody but me should have to swallow failure the size of an egg. I'm thirty-six today, which means I must've been about twenty-three when I went into the clinic. Thirteen years of broken rib dumb-luck. I'll be happy to kill myself after you, Val. Lucky number fifteen.

This responsibility was really easy at first. But after my fourth one, when I wrapped my loser fingers around your brother, Timmy's, neck, it hit me. These are *my* children. My arms turned to wrought iron and I got dizzy. Finding them on the Internet and meeting them is easy. Saving them from a lifetime of heartbreak and failure is the hard part.

YOU CAN'T BLOW YOURSELF TO SMITHEREENS ON AN EMPTY STOMACH

"THE CUL-DE-SAC WILL run red with the blood of the oppressors," Kevin McFadden said, slamming his fist on the breakfast table.

"Not on an empty stomach it won't," said his mom, Tammy, sloshing a bowl of Lucky Charms on the table and kissing her boy's hair.

"Ha," laughed George, his father. "The Great Satan is shaking in his shoes, slugger."

Kevin started wearing his *freedom mask* to breakfast a month ago. It made Tammy sweat a little. This was the most important meal of the day, and she didn't want her son looking like the Skoal Bandit. Besides, how can a boy eat Pop Tarts with that red bandanna wrapped around his face?

She gave up arguing about the facial wear and his new friends weeks ago. "*Mom*," Kevin would protest. "You don't understand kids my age. We don't want the Dictator's Army conquering America. This is what kids do today. We wear bandannas; we take to the streets; we bomb Iraqi motorcades for our freedom." Kevin's voice grew a note higher on the Whiny Scale every time this topic came up.

Tammy tried explaining how the invasion might be a good thing. Maybe the strategic destruction of shopping malls and baseball stadiums was a blessing. God knows sixteen-year old boys could use a little discipline. Groundings never worked, so maybe tyranny would shape him up, she hoped.

But try explaining that to a kid who comes down the cul-de-sac every day with the blood of oppressors staining his brand new fifty-dollar jeans.

"Kevin, just how do you expect to eat through your freedom bandanna?" She asked with a painfully clenched jaw.

"How can I eat anything while our land is being over-run with foreigners? They want to rape our country of its in-expensive fast food and outlet malls." He slammed his fist on the table again. "And I demand to know why!" He paused. She could hear his nose sniffing behind the red and white pattern. "Unless you're making bacon. Is that bacon?"

"Easy Kev," his dad piped up, chopping the boy's protest off like the head of an Iraqi advertising executive. Which, according to George's newspaper, was happening a lot out in the streets. Especially since it was open harvest on America's biggest resource: marketing secrets. "Your mom just wants to see you have a good morning before you and your Freedom Cell go off liberating all day." George's voice always cooled off family drama, whether it was extending curfew, dealing with unfinished chores or a suspicious col-lection of human skulls buried in the backyard.

"I know," he mumbled, unknotting the scarf. "I'm sorry, Mom."

A cracked grin spread over Tammy's mouth. Maybe a dictatorship rich in oil is exactly what this family needs, she thought.

"But I'm so furious," Kevin said, scooping in ce-real. "There's this big suicide bombing later this morning, an Iraqi motorcade is stopping at the IHOP—some photo opportunity to show how safe things are here. Sitting ducks, you know? Benny down the street told me, like, six other cells are involved."

"Golly, I bet that'll get their attention, Son. But you can't blow yourself to smithereens on an empty belly," said George, opening his newspaper with a snap and refocusing his attention.

"That's just it, Dad. Mikey Medved says my hatred for the invaders isn't pure enough. God, he's the worst Freedom Cell leader ever!"

"Oh, how is Mikey?" Tammy asked. "If you see his parents, tell them we say, 'hi.'"

"According to him, only those with perfect souls may kill themselves in the name of America. Only the seventeen-year-old guys are ready, he says. I mean, by the time I'm old enough there won't be any Wal-Marts or Costcos left to save!"

"Well, I don't see what all the fuss is about," Tammy said, starting to clang the dirty dishes around the sink. "Personally, I'm sick of driving all the way to the VFW hall to vote every November. Can't someone else make these choices? It hurts my head." She stopped and stared at a patch of burnt black bricks and melted plumbing that used to be the Griffins' house. Their cul-de-sac was accidentally bombed by friendly fire last week. The opposite side of the street was a buzz cut of prefabricated homes with smolders of smoke still rising from the char. "I'd *like* one ruler to make all our decisions. I can't wait until they help set up our own dictatorship in America."

"Mom, you're so out of touch." He stood and knotted the bandanna around his head again. "You just don't get it."

George looked at his watch and gagged on his bacon. "Well, Family," he said, picking up his briefcase, "the Indian casino isn't going to run itself this morning. I better get going."

He scruffed his son's hair and kissed Tammy on the cheek. Surprised, she swung around from the dishes and knocked his briefcase to the ground.

George McFadden's dirty secret spilled across the floor. His patriotic cheeks blushed as red as his son's freedom bandanna.

In his case, split open like a watermelon—six bundles of C-4 explosives, a detonator and a bandanna spun to a rest on the linoleum next to a map leading to the IHOP.

41

JESUS TOAST

I SAW BURNT toast that looked like Jesus.

Mother Theresa was an oil stain in the garage.

Buddha was a puddle of melted ice cream.

But I never saw anything like my sister Carmen's wedding cake.

Claude was mad because lately my only visions were ex-boyfriends. I saw Steve—We dated from 1999-2001—in the knots of an oak tree. There was an omelet that had a Moses-like quality, but only turned out to be Gary the Hippie (1995-1996).

Claude said he's not the jealous type, but I don't buy it. My man stopped holding the door open for me, rubbing my feet and spilling red wine all over perfectly good couch cushions after we inspected the Immaculate Rust Stain. He wanted the Virgin Mary...not "Marty: The Guy Who Took My Virginity" (1983).

Confused? Let me lay it out for you. Say you spill coffee on your best white shirt. Where most see a splotchy brown mess that needs a trip to the dry cleaner, I see the Shroud of Turin. It's a gift for seeing things others can't.

Ok, you're with me, right? You looked smart; I had a feeling.

So, say your kid hits a golf ball against the garage window. Where you see it cracked all to hell and needing replaced, I see Ike Turner.

Now, let's bring both piles of shattered glass to my boyfriend. Guess which one Claude could turn into a profit?

Religious figures were our toast and jam. About once a year, you see something on the news concerning a tree branch that *sorta* grew into the shape of the Dali Lama. Or something even more ridiculous—Jesus on burnt toast comes to mind again. Chances are, my twisted eyeballs and Claude's thunder and lightning had something to do with it.

Well, if you're around the micro-media storm that follows one of these stories, you can connect the dots to figure someone is making a profit from this news. Sure, it's not a White House scandal or the rising price of oil, but soft news sells, baby. My visions were always the last item before the anchor signed off. A little sprinkle of sugar on top of the salmonella-sandwich that is the nightly news.

That was the X where the big bucks were buried. You don't need a psychic gift like mine to read that treasure map. Dan Rather shows Jesus Toast for ten seconds, and we sell it on eBay for a grand. That doesn't include shipping—a thousand bucks of pure profit, boys and girls.

Claude was my boyfriend and manager for almost five years. We mostly traveled around the South—Florida's a big one, Texas too. Where you see the Bible Belt, I see the Melted-Candle-that-looks-like-Hitler Belt.

As a little girl, I saw clouds shaped like Italy and mud puddles that looked like wine bottles. Nobody cared until a bunch of years back, daydreaming in choir practice, I mentioned how a burnt scrap of paper looked like Saint Peter. Soon enough, everybody was calling the neighbors over to take a peek. I don't know if anyone else could honestly see Saint Peter, but they sure acted like it.

A lot of, "Ohhhhh, ohhhh, *now* I see ol' Petey." Or, "Well, golly, I guess if you tip it on his ear, then, yeah, I do see the Pearly Gate-keeper himself."

Finally, some lady from the church's office offered me fifteen bucks for it. Well, duh, you and I see the same thing, I'll bet. Yep, that's a light bulb sizzling above my head so bright a woman needs sunglasses.

Things blossomed pretty naturally from that point. It's nothing but your average religious-visionary-meets-one-eyed-street-vendor/public-relations-wiz-kid love story. At the height of our powers, Claude and I owned a used van and rented apartments in Dallas and Orlando.

But I recently hit a stretch as dry as Jesus Toast without a pat of Pope John Paul butter. We were hungry and hurting for some publicity. Days of sitting around in our rented wicker furniture, waiting for my eyes to get back into gear, turned into weeks. Every time something promising came along, my peepers only saw a prison lineup of my past lovers.

If you're curious, I can tell you the exact date that my voodoo went sour. Seventy-eight days ago. Yep, my sister's wedding. Boy, you're good.

Carmen looked pretty enough in her white dress at that barn of a church. At least, I thought the bride looked good until the urge to strangle her overcame me as she waltzed down the aisle. I've seen a lot of crazy faces in unexpected places— Ronald Regan in a rotten pumpkin comes to mind—but none more than my oldest sister, Ruth, batting clean-up as Maid of Honor. I used to think Carmen and I were best friends. But I wasn't even asked to read, let alone stand beside her on the biggest day of her life. A day I have yet to experience, keep in mind. Needless to say, I was crushed. I don't know why my family acts so embarrassed about my job. It's a hell of a lot better than being a hairdresser. Carmen just won't admit it.

At the reception, I was so angry I could have lit a cigar with my stare. Claude and I took a walk through the cool night while I tried to blow off steam. My panic disappeared when he wrapped a warm arm around my shoulder and said he loved me.

Well, the stars were spinning like a kaleidoscope that night, and my heart was seeing some visions of its own, let me tell you.

That bliss lasted about as long as a sneeze, because the steam blew through the ceiling when the wedding cake caught my eye. Two waiters carried it on a tray. It shook back and forth like a skyscraper in a hurricane. That thing was stacked as tall as a midget and white as a wall socket, real pretty.

But you know the way fancy frosting leaves a jet stream across the cake—one of those trails telling you where the knife's been? Well, under the hot lights of that cramped Elk's Lodge, Carmen's big wedding dessert was spread up and down and inside out with those marks. So much so that what I saw in that frosting, right below the mini bride and groom, made me drop my pink champagne.

I called it a sign. Claude called me drunk. Unfortunately, I think I was right.

My man tried to synthetically produce our little "miracles" after the wedding. I can still picture Claude standing on the dining room table in our Dallas apartment a few weeks ago, Thanksgiving turkey roasting in the oven and filling the whole place with that smell, and him holding a gravy boat dripping with brown gunk. "Just picture the Prophet Mohammad," he said.

"But I don't know what he looks like," I said. I wanted to flip Claude the bird, but lucky for him I'm a lady.

"Nobody does. That's the beauty part." A big grin formed a ways under his eye patch. "As long as you say it, people will buy it. I'm going to start pouring on the tablecloth. You tell me when your vision appears."

I didn't want to hurt Claude's feelings, but it was pretty obvious this wasn't going to work. Bless his heart. He tried hard, though.

When the gravy gelled, the only Muslim face that appeared was a guy named Khalid (1988). He was less of a boyfriend than a one-night fling, you know. But he had a poster of Muhammad Ali over his bed, which I said was a pretty crazy coincidence.

Claude disagreed.

Five tablecloths later, he quit. One *kind* of looked like Elvis, but I think my mind was playing tricks.

Oh wait. I didn't mention Elvis?

The King. Mr. *Aloha from Hawaii*. In short, the

bottom left-hand corner of my Holy Trinity of visions—the King, Jesus and Mary.

I met Claude out in front of Graceland. Memphis that time of year was sunny and brutally humid, with the smell of barbecuing wood smoke sticking to everything like sweat. This was my Pierre era (2001-2002). Funny I should mention him; I recently spotted Pierre as a coffee stain at the bottom of my favorite mug. Huge nose; couldn't miss it.

Short on bus fare back home to Atlanta and stuck in Memphis, I spent my last dollar on French fries at some grease trap diner—Hunka Hunka Burnin' Stove. If I was going to survive for a while without eating, I figured it was time to stock up on vegetables. I sprayed enough ketchup to paint a house, assuming tomatoes were a good source of vitamins. Well, at the bottom of my plate was what I call my first honest-to-goodness miracle. Little old me stuck in big Memphis with poverty breathing down my blouse, and who pops in to say, "hi," but Elvis Aaron Presley.

The place was cramped, and the air conditioning was busted. The entire dining room was sweating like it was an IRS audit. "Excuse me," I grabbed the waitress' attention, "but does this look like someone famous?" I said, pointing to the puddle of Heinz on my plate.

"Looks like a mess, young lady," she said through a stiff fog of K-Mart perfume and a frown. "You gonna order anything but fries?"

This was the revelation I needed. This woman changed my life. I should find her and repay that waitress with a slice of Jesus Toast or something.

"Don't you think it looks a little like Elvis?" I said. "You know, Fat Elvis."

She paused, squinted and dropped the plate of meatloaf she was taking to the booth behind me. "Well by George, I'd say you're right." Her mood changed for the better, like we went to high school together. "I didn't see it until you pointed it out. Look, there's his hair and that rhinestone jumpsuit. Hey, Cal, lookey what we found!"

The keys to my castle were carved out of ketchup. Turned out as soon as you plant a thought in someone's head and give them a cheat sheet, nine-times-out-of-ten they'll see it. Or they'll pretend in order not to sound stupid. No matter how dull or boring, everyone wants a little magic in their life.

So I carried that plate down the street to Graceland as careful as the cake waiters at Carmen's wedding.

Elvis had a wrought iron fence around his property, and it looked like the White House sorta, if you stare at it long enough.

The sidewalk was splattered with people getting their pictures taken in front of the gate and squirrelly looking dudes selling Elvis memorabilia: dolls, shot glasses, posters. Which is exactly where Claude makes his appearance. He sold children's rhinestone jumpsuits, so your chubby little tyke could look just like Fat Elvis.

Quickly, a couple with a creative imagination where matters of ketchup were concerned offered to buy the plate for fifty-bucks—more than enough for bus fare. Just then, this guy, who wound up becoming my boyfriend, Claude (2002-last week), stepped up. "I'll give you a hundred," he said.

In a snap, a bidding war erupted like a Beirut firefight. The more shouting, the more Presley-heads who came by, the more people who saw Fat Elvis carved out of ketchup, the more money was thrown at me. For three hundred bucks, a housewife from Ohio walked away with a chipped plate full of pureed tomatoes.

"Who'd you say that ketchup was supposed to look like?" Claude asked me afterward when we shared a popsicle and got matching sunburns.

I was speechless. I mean, *duh.*

"I didn't see shit in that plate. You just looked like a girl who could use a hand." His smile sent stars up my spine. It still does, though I haven't so much as seen Claude grin in months.

Well, next thing you know my heart is a melted puddle

and we're mixing my *gift* and his *gab* all across the county. Our biggest sale, with the help of a quick spot on FOX News, was a lemon meringue pie that looked like Donald Trump, especially the haircut. I bought the pie for five and sold it over the Internet for three-grand. You're smart; do the math.

Remember how I said nine-out-of-ten people see it? Well, there's always one skeptic. Some people, no matter how exposed they are, keep their eyes snapped shut. Or maybe they just don't *want* to see. These are always the first people to break the Easter Bunny news to kids. If I were to place some bets, I'd put up a hundred Donald Trump pies that says Claude never saw it. He didn't see Darth Vader; he didn't see Mary or Jesus or Elvis—he just saw a few dollars. That was until my sister's wedding cake came into the picture. A grown man has never been so shaky, so frightened, in all Earth's history.

"Would you look at that?" I said about two seconds before I dropped my pink champagne in front of that tall white cake. "Do you see what I see?"

"Jesus Christ," Claude said, half out of breath, tugging at the tie knot around his neck. "That looks like me and you up on the cake frosting. Hot God, it even has my eye patch!"

Well, that's when the shit hit the fan, or the pink champagne hit the floor, whichever you prefer.

After we cleaned up the glass and the bubbly, I whispered to him, "I think that's a sign, a miracle. *You* saw it, Claude. You never see it." My heart was pumping pink champagne at this point, full of girlish ideas of happiness. "Let's get married. We should be on our own wedding cake."

He looked like he caught a cannonball in the stomach; his jaw was unhinged. "We'll talk about it later, babe."

You've been doing a hell of a job keeping up, so I don't need to explain that our *talk* never came. I stopped seeing Bible heroes and Heartbreak Hotelers. After the wedding, I just saw all the guys I should have married...all the guys that proposed to me. Well, except for Khalid. Who knows where he came from?

PANDEMIC JONES

1

"I WANT TO vomit on you so bad right now," she said, muffled behind the electric yellow biohazard suit. Her eyes were wet. I still can't smell dry plastic without thinking of her.

Toko's personality changed faster than her racing pulse. "Come on, take this thing off. I've got another couple minutes. Just give me a kiss goodbye." Her eyes changed, too. They were sweet and knowing, like our rare quiet moments together.

I looked at the whirring computer screen of bars and charts over her shoulder under the dim lights. According to the screen, her heart rate was shooting up, as was her blood pressure.

"This should all be over soon," the doctor said, trying to pull me away without luck. My shoes squealed against the floor.

"We'll kill you!" she snarled. I couldn't get mad. It boned me like a fish, pulled everything out in a slow shot. "You piece of shit, be a man! Stand up for me if you love me!"

When she got into screaming jags, the clear faceplate fogged up.

This is the chance you take dating a walking bomb.

2

Reiser Pharmaceuticals' office was a white-collar ant colony in a tall plate glass building near Capitol Hill. I'd been there for about three years as a marketing assistant. My job was to go through every piece of advertising material—thousands of brochures, ads, pens and stationary—to ensure our products all had the little ® symbol after the name. After eight hours of squinting under fluorescent lights and circling the symbols in red ink, my mind was so murky I couldn't remember how to tie my shoes.

We gossiped about coworkers, but most people focused their whispers on the term, "FTF." Company terms had the scales removed. Face-to-Face Marketers. If somebody could have shortened Face-To-Facers down to something shorter than FTF, she would have been given a corner office. FTFs were easy to spot. Our business casual outfits were just different shades of gray against their suits. Black pants for guys, black skirts for ladies, white shirt, green blazer, green tie. Like real estate agents outside these walls, but inside they were Hollywood cool.

Toko started her job long after I'd arrived. She wasn't hard to notice at first. A splash of paint like that sticks out pretty well against corporate beige.

She came by my department twice a day, pushing a mail cart. The first day I stood up to watch her leave, her hair was fire hydrant orange. She wore a blouse with screen-printed bombs running down the sleeves. Her stockings were split apart along the back of her legs like someone chased her with a razor blade.

We didn't speak for a long while. She was just the hot Asian mail girl. When I heard the mouse squeaks from her cart's wheels, I'd find a reason to leave my cube. More coffee, send a fax, pick up a file. Twice a day for weeks I'd walk past and give the eye. She never as much flashed my shoes a glimpse as she dug through the mail.

"Hey, I'm Crutch. You do the mail right?" I left my hand dangling in front of her. It got cold and lonely hanging out there.

It was months after she'd started pushing that cart, and we were sitting next to each other in the company auditorium. "You're in Marketing. Crutchfield, you get a shit-ton of mail, man." Her nails were painted black with a racing stripe of neon purple down the center of each. She smiled like she knew something I didn't.

"Wow, I didn't know you ever noticed me up there." My shoulders tensed and my throat was some dry desert snake hole.

A blindingly clean room was filling up around us. Basic chatter and gossip fed from person to person.

"The mailman knows all."

"Mailperson, I think you mean." My shaky fingers tried to playfully tap her arm and flirt without success. I felt neutered the moment my skin touched hers.

"Whatever you say...*Crutch.*"

Two FTFs stood at the front of the room, patiently waiting for the place to fill. Seats were saddled, and I looked around me. Everyone stared at the green jackets glimmer-eyed, like kids meeting Santa. I waited for someone to ask for an autograph.

FTFs weren't really seen as much as they were talked about. Rumors, corporate ghosts. When you saw one, you sent a detailed email to your coworkers: "I saw one chewing a toothpick."

"I hear they all drive BMWs."

"I heard they can't talk, that they're some kind of genetic experiment."

"I'd heard that, too. Human guinea pigs."

Human Resources never, and I mean ever, called to tell you about any opening at Reiser. Normally, if you wanted to look at a new position, it was buried in some online company database. But like everyone else in the room, I got a call the week prior about this meeting regarding a few openings in sales, and would I be interested in a big increase in pay, benefits, company car...my ears mudslid into static and hisses of happiness after that.

3

They told us Face-to-Face marketing was a mushroom cloud in the industry. "Blowing up huge. You can see it from a hundred miles in all directions," the male FTF said.

"We started it. You know those commercials urging patients to take control or bug their doctor for specific medicine instead of simply taking the professional's word for it?" The woman FTF made a *well duh* kind of face.

"This is the next logical step," they said. "Go out to the people; hear their stories; preach the gospel." Those words sent a wire from my toes to my neck and tied electric knots along the way. The telegraph made my eyes pop open, and I started climbing it like a rope.

"You're all here for a reason," the girl said. "You come highly recommended by your supervisors and fit a strict set of guidelines we need in our field agents."

It sounded vaguely cultish. I shifted from ass cheek to cheek, my pants coiling tighter. But at the same time, I was flattered.

"Look around, I bet you won't see one wedding ring. In fact, I guarantee it," the man in a green jacket said.

"And," the girl said picking up the ball, "you won't see anyone over thirty here. Funny coincidence, huh?" They both looked into our eyes when they spoke. Like paid professional speakers.

"Not really. This job is tough. Field agents might have to put in long hours and go on the road to all sorts of places. Kim, where were you last week?"

"Oh, God. San Diego, I think," the woman in a black skirt and green tie said. "Yeah, I was thinking Rio, but that was the week before. It's hard to keep track." She delivered a killer smile and a modest shrug.

A couple guys in front of me tagged elbows and grumbled happily. They made me suspicious; they made me wonder what was happening.

"We like field agents in their twenties. You guys have the attitude we want. You're hungry. You're not lazy like your middle-aged bosses. You make your own luck.

That's what we love."

The speech went on for another forty minutes. After they were done, they said anyone who wasn't interested in making six-figures and moving out of their shitty apartment could take the rest of the day off. "Go back to your boring job tomorrow," the man said with a laugh.

I always felt guilty about cutting out early, so I stayed and took the mandatory personality test. Imagine a logic and ethics juggernaut like the LSAT, pour on gasoline, light it and fill it out in a dark closet. That was the FTF personality test.

4

When the meeting was over, I instantly noticed the wild spikes of orange hair that bobbed a few feet ahead of me on the sidewalk. Toko's skirt fit like a tunicate. Twice a day I got my fill, but this was the first time that day. I almost didn't want to spoil my view by talking. The afternoon was cool, with sun shooting between tree branches when the leaves shuffled in the breeze.

"So, do you think you aced it or what?" I wanted to stab myself in the throat.

"Uh, sure. Who cares, you know?" the mail girl replied.

"Yeah, I was just kidding. Just a dumb joke."

"Right. I'm getting a drink. You want one?"

She drank two shots of whiskey before I had half a beer gone. In a basement pub, under a Greek restaurant, she sanded off some of her hard edges.

"I feel comfortable here. I can just hide out. I like that feeling. Invisibility. Invulnerability." Her eyes were dark and took bites at my heart. All I could think was not to say some dumb shit.

"Jeez, I feel stupid, but I still don't have your name," I said, gulping wet beer down the dry snake hole.

She looked over my shoulder. "So, what do you think the real deal is with those guys?"

"Huh?"

She juggled fifteen different thoughts. "Toko. It's Toko. That's Japanese, and no, I wasn't born there," she said like she's delivered it so often she should print out a business card. Toko grabbed my mug and took a slurp. "I hear they do experiments. Shit like people go up to their floor, but nobody ever comes down."

"That sounds unlikely. I've worked here for three years and…"

"I'm curious. What if they're just testing funky drugs on us? Doping us up."

"That's not reasonable. I think it's just sales. Just another way for Reiser to be sleazy. Did you read that company-wide email today? Restless Leg Syndrome is a big problem. Thank God we have the answer." I wanted to lay down with a stomach cramp when she didn't laugh at my joke.

"Maybe, Crutch." She blossomed her eyes, making fun of me. "But it seems reasonable that they'd want young, unattached guinea pigs. No one'll miss me when I overdose on the cure for Restless Leg Syndrome."

"How do they know if we have restless legs?" I eased a bit and smiled. "Your legs look well rested."

"I bet they give it to us first." She started nibbling on a fingernail. "No big deal. Like I said, no one'll miss me."

"I'd miss seeing you do the mail everyday." Some embarrassed part of my brain said suicide would be a good idea any time here.

She finished my beer and wiped her mouth with a sleeve. In a beam of street-level window light her hair flamed-out yellow, then deep red.

"Let's go back to my place. I'm just around the corner."

I followed her wire-hanger thin legs around the block. She marched with determination, spinning around executives on cell phones and their bruising shoulders, flipping quarters into a few coffee cans in front of homeless guys, sort of skipping down the street. I tried to lasso a little of that energy and keep up.

She lived in a studio, a cramped closet four stories over the buzz and honking of the street. When the door was closed, she kicked a pile of dirty laundry out of the way and popped a CD in the stereo. "Christ, I love Iggy Pop. So sexy."

She turned around, grabbed the back of my skull and kissed. The Stooges record came to life in max-volume vibrations through her speakers as she undid my shirt buttons.

I blew my wad by the beginning of *TV Eye.*

On the floor, my back ached from her thin mattress. I huffed embarrassed breaths, wondering how long before she tossed me out, naked into the street.

"Cumming is so overrated," she said, kicking my shoulder. "What, are we in high school? Who gives a shit, right?" My embarrassment disappeared after watching her give me a smile. My legs tingled.

I had no clue what to say. She was out of my league, and the last five minutes of kissing and all-too-brief sex were out of my zip code. I had no business with her.

The sun must have been setting. Her room was sherbet orange with light. I panicked and made pillow talk. "What's that tattoo on your hip mean?"

"Forget you saw that thing, Crutch." She rolled over. "Do you get high?"

Naked, she stood and grabbed a metal pipe from her bookshelf.

"Seriously," I said. "I've never seen a tattoo like that before."

She clicked her lighter, and the room filled with burning rope stink. "Knock it off, or get out," she said handing me a Zippo and the pipe.

"Is that a snake wrapped around a hammer or a Rorschach blot?"

Her voice beat my skull with frustration: "God, fine! It's the Lemon of Pink Society."

"What the hell does that mean?" I said, wiping my penis off with a white sock.

"It's like a club, okay? A small, private club."

"Like a sorority?"

"Get your clothes on before I get pissed. I said knock it off." She turned her back, exposing a tiny ass. "Are you pleased, Inspector Gadget?" Her voice was small and vulnerable.

She gave me enough time to slip into my underwear before I was hopping, one foot in my pants, down her hallway.

5

My answering machine blinked when I came home. Don't report to my usual floor, it said. Come up to the same meeting room as today. Bring a notepad.

The next morning, I was first to the auditorium. I even beat the green jackets. It was open and lonesome there. Fresh coffee smells filled the air as a janitor slowly scrubbed the dry erase board clean. "Crutch, you look lonely," Toko said, suddenly appearing. "You're not going to cry if I sit next to you, right? Start telling me your mom didn't hug you enough?"

"Listen, about yesterday." My heart kicked against my ribs; it pumped gallons.

"Aw shit, don't start," she said, crossing her hammerlock thighs. "Do you have some sort of mental defect where you sleep with someone and then try to piss her off every second afterward?" She gave me a wicked glance. "Maybe mommy didn't hug you enough."

"I just wanted to," I said, catching my breath.

Both greens from the day before walked in. "Greetings, finalists," the girl said.

Toko stabbed me with an elbow. "Relax. It was fun.

56

We should do it again sometime."

The first ten minutes of their speech was blurred, muted. *Again sometime.* My leg shook.

"You two are the cream of the crop," the man, Chet, said. He ushered us out of our seats with excited hand waves. "Nobody else in this entire building, this entire corporation, locked into our qualifications like you guys."

"Come on. You've got a lot of learning to do," green jacket Kim said.

We looked at each other. My eyes warm and already in some dim hope for love, even though I knew it'd never work. Toko's eyes were cold as Siberian gulags.

Paperwork. Mountains of signatures and initials. Force-fed; no time to read. When we signed by the last red arrow, Kim and Chet shook our hands. "Congratulations. Welcome to the big leagues."

The research lab tour was brief, lots of stainless steel and white walls. Lots of black and green computer screens. Lots of guys wearing protective masks and medieval-thick gloves. The clean sting of bleach filled my nose. "You guys'll get more of Research later," green jacket man said. "More than you'll ever want."

In the woman's office, we watched a PowerPoint. "Research," she said, "is the most difficult part of sales. We put thousands of hours into market research when we release a product." She leaned against the wall, crossed her legs. "Viophendren is a great example. Don't know it? You'll become an expert in a few weeks. Chet, how many man-hours did we put into Market Research before we turned the sales team loose?"

"Oh, wow, rough guess: sixteen-thousand. About four years worth."

We had lunch alone in the employee break room.

"Wow, this is going fast. My head's spinning," I said.

"You crack me up," Toko said, funeral serious. "God, did you move here from Idaho? Do you sit on the porch and whittle for fun?"

"I'm from San Jose." I curled my toes into a fist. "I get it, ha. You got me on the ropes. Bravo."

"Let's get another drink after work."

"Do you want to know a crazy fact?" green jacket Kim asked. I was suddenly hungry, since I couldn't force myself to take a bite during lunch. "You two are the healthiest people at Reiser Pharmaceuticals. That's what you guys had over everyone. Crutch, have you ever seen the inside of a hospital?"

"My grandma was real sick with lupus and we visited…"

The woman's office was a lot like the marketing department, I thought. Nicer view. I could see the river from my seat. But the furniture sucked as bad as mine. She had the same non-offensive nature prints hanging on the wall as my old boss. Where was the mystery of the green jackets? Where was the high-wire act, snorting blow off hookers juggling fire?

"Let me help. *No*, you haven't. Toko, you too."

Chet stepped in. "You're even better than him. Not even a flu bug in your twenty-three years. Unreal. That's what we like to see. Christ, know those stiff shirts in research? That shit makes them do cartwheels."

I took a barrel-load breath. Everything was spoken in smiley-faced riddles. I wished I remembered a notepad to jot some of it down.

"Listen, we might have led you guys on a bit. But we only did it with the best intentions," Kim said. "FTF means a lot of things. It means going into the field."

"Into hospitals," Chet said.

"Into PTA meetings."

"To drug conventions."

"To large churches."

"It means going wherever people who care about their health are."

"I don't think that's a lie," Toko said. She stiffened in her chair, and I stared at her flat breasts for a quick moment.

"No, it's not," Chet said, nodding like Toko was catching on fast. "You're going to be sent to the masses. Thing is, while you might be asking them how we can best treat everyone, ah." He smacked his lips.

The woman slid into home. "You'll be giving them something else."

"I'm not following," Toko said as we looked at one another.

"*Giving* them?" I said. My mind focused on what they were proposing and away from breaking my thirty-second sex record for the first time.

"Ok, okay, hypothetical time," she said, pulling out a glossy brochure. "Fluxinal. Take a look."

Glossy shots of kids and grandparents on a playground on the cover. Dad baking pies on the inset. No pictures of pills. No pictures of prescription bottles. No shots of doctors.

Toko started scratching the back of her hand like there was an itch she couldn't relieve.

"Know what Fluxinal is for?" Chet asked, locking on Toko.

"Huh," she chuckled, "not the slightest." She gave an unsure, unconfident look that half-shocked me. Her fingernails were leaving pink streaks along the back of her hand now.

"Problem is," green jacket Kim said, "nobody does. It's our lowest selling product. We'd axe it, but production has two-point-nine million units sitting in a warehouse in Dayton, OH. Know what kind of loss that is?"

"Fluxinal," Chet said, snapping back the brochure, "cures whooping cough. Cures it for about two dollars and thirty-three cents a pill. So that warehouse adds up."

I raised my hand. "Do people still get the whooping cough? It sounds ancient, like Black Plague." I lowered my hand nervously.

"Start watching the news. It's coming back in a big way. I think we've got outbreaks scheduled for Wichita, Boca Raton and St. Louis."

The FTF world was a game of Boggle. It was jumbling around, spelling new words I'd never seen before.

"Our agents," Kim said, closing her door, "collect data." Her face relaxed into a smile. "But they also spread the virus. That's where the fat sales commissions come in."

"That's where vacations in Tahiti come in," Chet said.

"That's where *summer home* becomes a word you'll use."

"You'll be seeing about thirty-five cents on each pill you help sell. Think of that one, Crutch."

6

I out-drank Toko at the bar. I was in a hurry to numb myself to the things I'd learned that day. The lights were dim again, which allowed my mind to wander.

That night, I was as short in bed as the last time. Toko was right; cumming is overrated.

"I don't think I'm going back tomorrow," I said, one hand tenderly smoothing out her orange rag of hair, kissing her neck, my hips stinging from her thin mattress lying on the hardwoods. I stuffed my nose into her hair, trying to erase the musty smell of her old laundry around the room.

"Good god, are you scared of *everything*? You're like a kitten."

"You can't tell me that wasn't weird. What the hell was all that?"

"Just pushy salesmanship." Toko's stood and started digging through the piles of clothes. "Would you believe free advertising, maybe?"

"The whole operation just seems fishy. Maybe I can go back to my old job." Her white cat rubbed against my leg, purring, as I searched for a sock.

"You're gonna stick it out. You're going to wake up, pick up those clothes on the floor and walk in that door with me." Her voice was so sharp my posture straightened.

She flipped on the radio and slipped on a robe. Her thigh hung out the slit. She crinkled her nose and sprayed a small perfume bottle into the air until her room smelled like honeysuckle.

Pulling on my pants, I was overcome with the urge to try and beat my record again. "Yeah, maybe you've got a good argument there." I grabbed her hips. Maybe cumming isn't overrated, I thought.

The city was winding down outside her window. A neon purple fog filled the sky, and quiet tire-on-asphalt traffic found its way up four stories. She turned on the eleven o'clock news.

"Today's top stories: Fighting in Syria leaves eleven dead. The DOW tumbles for the third straight day in a row. Mysterious outbreaks of Whooping cough across the country. And the Floredine Liberation Army, back after decades in the shadows?"

"Hot shit!" She struggled from my grip. "Did you hear that?" She turned up the radio and came back to me. "I can't wait for work tomorrow."

We kissed so hard my teeth hurt. Suddenly, I couldn't wait either.

7

Months flew by. Diseases crawled through our bodies like blood transfusions. Malaria, Measles, Mumps, Rubella. I slept with a woman puffing out things like Spanish Hog Flu and Green Typhoid with each sexy, humid breath.

Huge commissions stumbled in. After a few months, I had a bankwad thick as a dictionary. I coughed aching, fat hacks. But my bank account and libido pushed forward.

Toko and I moved into a new condo together. The place was in my name, but she split the payments. It was on the tenth floor with a view of the river, ceilings as tall as a barn roof, bamboo floors and a big bed that kicked the shit out of that lumpy futon mattress Toko laid on her studio's floor.

Like most new adventures, things started off great. I cleaned up the messes; she was a decent cook, and my record in bed leaped near the one-and-a-half minute mark. But little droplets of peculiarity quickly formed around Toko.

Every Wednesday night she was gone. A few times I tried to stay awake to greet her, but Toko never made it back before I passed out. She was always next to me in bed when I woke up, though.

"It's my stitch and bitch group," she told me. I swallowed her cue ball-sized story all the way down my throat. "We just get some drinks, do some knitting and end up chatting most of the night." I'd never noticed as much as a crocheted potholder or a knitting needle around our place.

Work cracked down hard on us. Sending escorts on every trip. It happened after a Young Republicans convention in Boston. Toko was supposed to spread Severe Tanno-Bronchitis, a strain six times as harmful as old-fashioned bronchitis. Instead, two hundred young right-wingers never left Boston General. A flood of shaking, epileptic men and women poured into the hospital. Brains soggy, half-a-step from a flat line.

Advanced Mad Cow Disease, some newspapers speculated. Unheard of. A predatory strain that takes only a matter of hours, instead of the normal decades, to effect the brain, another reported.

We were hustled back to D.C., back to the labs. Toko had accidentally caught her first non-work disease: a staph infection. Mixed together with the bronchitis, like ammonia and bleach, she was a walking pandemic.

But she already knew that.

The office quarantined her. Three weeks later, she was back to her old self, a little gray in the cheeks, though.

The rivets popped out of our new life one Wednesday night. The local hospital woke me up with a call. Toko was in the ER. I was her emergency contact.

A dark cloud of black floated in the lounge. Nearly a dozen women, black t-shirts and horrible, cornea-melting stares. Each had a red bandanna around her forehead. Rosie the Gothic Riveter.

I waited for a doctor. An hour, two, three. These frightening women stomped and grunted all around me. I wondered if they were a biker gang. Maybe one of their riders was in an accident.

The newspaper barely kept me awake. The Floredine Liberation Army had been sending shadowy threats to the government again, just like it had thirty years prior.

The story clicked a switch in my head. That evening, when Toko was out, I watched the news. The Floredine Liberation Army story was buried between striking teachers and the weather report. Pictures of the army from the 70s flashed across the screen. Militant women dressed in black, red bandannas around their faces, shouted threats to Jimmy Carter from their secret bunker. Oil dependency, capitalism crushing souls…the same thing they threatened now, I realized.

My breath freeze dried as I realized I was knee deep in the army swamp. Was I was lucky to be alive?

The doctor walked in, possibly saving my life. "Toko had a seizure. Is she on medication for any sickness?"

"Um, not that I'm aware," I gulped. If Doctor Lyles only knew.

8

An orange tangle of hair crept from under the blankets when I walked in her room. I gave her a soft kiss on the head, and she woke. We stared at one another for another hour before the hospital released her. Her dripping IV was the only movement in the room.

I wheeled Toko out of the hospital. A nurse handed me her belongings in a clear plastic Zip-Loc.

"Here's her wallet, her shoes and what's left of her shirt." The contents pressed against the bag like algae in a fish bowl. "It had to be cut off."

Swimming around the shoes and the wallet were tatters of a black t-shirt.

"Oh, I'll take that," Toko said, in a weak but sharp voice. She pulled her hand from under her blanket. The backside of the bag was a flash of red bandanna.

I turned back, but the black shirts had disappeared. The waiting area was all white walls, harsh lights and empty chairs.

The next morning, she bounced around the house like nothing had happened. "Thanks for picking me up," she said sweetly. "I owe you something special." She wrapped arms around me and let her hands do the talking.

"You have some explaining to do," I said, removing her hand from my zipper. "What is all this bandanna shit? Who were those women? What..." I breathed heavy. "What's going on? I don't feel like I know you."

A headache electrified every pulse of blood through my head as I looked around our place. The stunning morning light came through the windows and shimmered off the river below. That light rain on dry concrete smell came with it. I picked at one of the many boxes we still hadn't unpacked.

She walked around silent, poured a glass of water, sat and drank half, then spoke. "Can you keep a secret?"

9

There was a wobble in my vision, and the sun made my headache worse. My foot caught on a box as I stomped toward her. "You're what?"

"Honey, it's for a good cause. It's for our future." Toko had never called me "honey." Her eyes and frown made an ashamed expression. I'd never seen her close to that emotion, and it scared me.

Beads of sweat formed on my forehead. "We need to be at work in an hour." I popped my knuckles nervously. I turned my back and went into the bedroom. The echoing sound of my shoes on our hardwood floors left my heart feeling empty.

"Look at our world, at our country." Her voice snagged me, and my feet stopped. "It's falling apart because of this government." The hard-ass Toko was gone. All that was left was this soft, helpless human. For the first time, I had a sense she was being honest. "Wars, hurricane disasters, record unemployment, government corruption…Crutch, I could go on all day. It needs to be stopped. It needs a bullet in the head."

"So…" The words were heavy and made my jaw muscles ache. "What, you're killing the president?"

When I turned around, she was scratching the back of her hand. "No, I mean *all* the powers that be. The Senate, the Congress, the judges and yeah, the President. A freakin' clearinghouse." Her eyes were bright and excited, like she didn't suffer a severe medical trauma last night.

"I don't get it." I shook my head and eyed the door, the knob, how many steps it would take to run away and wash my hands of this mess. But some sense of responsibility stopped me.

She wrapped her thin arms around my neck. "Okay, God…they'd kill me if they found out. YOU CANNOT TELL A SOUL THIS." She punctuated the sentence with a tight kiss.

"Toko, you're scaring me," I said, clutching her hand.

"I'm a walking chemistry set," she said with a half-smile and a *whoops* kind-of laugh.

"Our job is weird, but in the long run we're helping people. Just like Chet said, you know?" I needed to take a leak, but the bathroom felt miles away.

"No, more than just work." Open veins of emotion uncovered themselves in her voice.

I breathed through my nose. My jaw was on lockdown. Toko's honeysuckle perfume smelled sour now.

"I'm in the Floredine Liberation Army. Those were the leaders of the group you saw tonight. They've been experimenting with my body for a year. Mixing different cocktails of diseases, making stronger new ones."

"Toko, that's ridiculous. What are you really doing?"

"Tonight was a bad night," she whispered. "A bad cocktail. It's a long shot, but they got it all figured out." She treated me like I was dumb. Fury dropped a bomb on me.

"Figured what?" My angry voice echoed off the tall ceilings.

"Reiser has certain diseases in tiny petri dishes that no one knows about. We've got another girl on the inside. She tells us what's coming up, and our scientists do the code cracking. We're usually close. But I think they figured it out." She looked me straight in the eye, her black roots popping out under a blanket of orange spiky hair as raggedy as her story. "Just in time for the State of the Union address tonight."

Tiny mosaic pieces slid together in a stained glass painting, shiny and distorted, but clear enough for me to see. "Are you saying…"

"If it works, nobody will walk out of the capitol building alive, and our country can start completely over again. Take a mulligan."

10

Toko made me hustle to work. She was showing signs of weakness from the hospital. Her legs walked slower. Her head hung low and watched her shoes.

Reiser was the usual. She went into the lab, got her injection and was handed a stack of papers telling her where to go. Her plane was to leave at five in the afternoon.

They gave me my usual placebo shot in the ass.

"Go visit your mom in Vermont. Take a sick day," she said. "I don't know what's going to happen tonight. There could be rioting and fighting, who knows?"

"You're not doing this. You can't." I was driving us home. She was supposed to be packing. Stoplights stretched for silent hours.

"The wheels are in motion. I'm sorry. I love you," she said. "This world'll be a better place after this. Just wait."

"How do you think this is going to work? That place is Fort Knox on a night like this." Cars were honking at me to go; the light was green.

"The wheels are in motion, like I said. There are a couple senators who love their public so much they don't take the secure underground entrance. I give myself a shot in the arm, and I've got twenty minutes. Twenty minutes to cough on one of these guys as he jogs up the steps and waves to the crowd. Then the senator does all the hard work. It goes from one guy to the next, like a yawning fit in church. By the time they all sit down, packed in thick like a factory pig farm, it'll be running through three times over. After that, nothing can save them. There's no cure. Our country is born again. A new July Fourth." Her voice was so happy and proud it made my hands shake with fear.

11

Back at the office, Toko kicked against the restraints, and her biohazard suit steamed. She couldn't talk any more. Her insides were eaten up, boiling into pasta sauce. The Army was a couple molecules off on what Reiser had given her that afternoon. But those tiny molecules of carbon in a different direction turned her from a walking pandemic to a human time bomb.

One of the scientists had the State of the Union address on TV. The president rambled on for an hour about how important it is to keep fighting overseas.

I stood watching Toko explode, my heart filled with saltwater sting. Each ventricle popped like a fire hose. *This* is how my first love ends.

She made one last convulsion, and the clear faceplate smeared with bloody vomit. The computers and charts and monitors squeaked dead.

I rubbed my fingers against the plastic glove covering her hand. My eyes started to moisten, but I held it back.

Homeland Security spies don't cry, I told myself.

ME AND GERARDO DOWN
BY THE SCHOOLYARD

"SO, WE'RE ALL dying to know, Gerardo," my boss says, bounce-passing to some guy he assures me was huge in the 90s. "What's your next move? How are you gonna follow-up *Rico Suave*?"

The sun stings the back of my neck. A breeze blows the basketball net back and forth, but doesn't make this place any cooler. I'm sitting on a beach towel because this place smells like homeless people. Who knows what germs are on the concrete?

"If you're so curious," Gerardo says, "why haven't you called me since 1991?" He sinks a jumper. His baggy jeans and bare chest seem kind of dated. Gerardo looks like the dude on my dad's old Soundgarden CDs, but with shorter hair and a doo rag.

"Gerardo, buddy, you'll always be my first client. We'll share that...that *bond* forever." My boss lasers a glance to make sure I emphasize the last part in my notes. "But, hey, I had other acts to manage. Right Said Fred hit it so big, and then those Budweiser Frogs..." he throws his hands up the way he does when I bring him the wrong espresso. "...those little green bastards rocketed through the roof! I'm sorry, pal."

Gerardo dribbles in a lay-up. His bandana gets sweaty in the sun and slips back on his receding hairline. His stomach bounces like my gym teacher's boobs.

Is this where Gerardo lives? This neighborhood has more broken windows and cars on blocks than it does stray dogs. And I've counted a dozen mutts stumbling past since the basketball game started.

"Who is this kid, anyhow?" Gerardo palms the basketball and points it in my direction. "I thought it was just gonna be us."

I jump a little, proud to be noticed in a meeting for once. But my stomach also tightens, scared to get called on.

"This little guy here is my intern, Ben Lambers." My boss keeps talking while he digs food out of his back teeth with a finger. "It's his summer break from Deshler High School. He gets me coffee, shines my shoes and dictates everything I say…you know, intern shit."

"Hey kid," Gerardo says, sweat buttering his fleshy folds. "When *you* write a Latin-pop crossover hit that's ten years ahead of its time, don't have Irv manage your career."

"Hey now," Irv says, loosening his tie, then bricking a three-pointer. "Take it easy, will ya? Ben, don't write that down. Scratch it out."

I assume this is a test. I bite the end of my pen hard, debating and then write that down.

"So, to answer your question, Irv," Gerardo says, his eyes so big and sad, "my next move involves you, me and a courtroom."

"Bullshit," my boss says, spitting out a gulp of red Gatorade. "On what grounds?"

They both lock eyes and walk close to each other, meeting at the free throw line. I count at least three syringes Irv kicks out of his path along the way.

"Look, man, I don't want to get into details here. I thought we could talk man-to-man at this playground."

"Ben, go sit in the car, would ya?" my boss says. "Call my secretary. Tell her I need an acupuncture appointment scheduled today or something."

I nearly fall for his trick, but just scribble that down, too. I'm exhausted, but full of adrenaline. The music business is so exciting. I can't wait to tell my mom.

Gerardo breathes heavy and squints at Irv. His voice gets really sharp when he says: "Jesus Jones and I were talking a few days ago. Turns out he still runs around with the guys in EMF. And their drummer plays racquetball with

Biz Markie every Tuesday. And then Biz saw the guy from Digital Underground at a garage sale. And guess who they were talking about?"

These names sound familiar in a *VH1 Where-Are-They-Now* kind of way. But I'm guessing this is some old-man code-speak. Kind of like when Mom used to spell out when I had an appointment with the D-O-C-T-O-R. I pay close attention; this seems important.

"Who?" Irv turns and dribbles the ball. His hands are unsteady.

At this angle, I realize Gerardo has his jeans pulled down so his white boxer shorts puff out. I nearly tell him he's having a fashion malfunction, but decide I'd miss some dictation.

"Well, Mr. Humpty Dance is in a stay-at-home-dads playgroup with Right Said Fred. And, as you may or may not recall, Right Said Fred was the best man at my third wedding."

"Big deal. Are you gonna talk all day or shoot?"

Gerardo misses a foul shot. The wind dies, and the only thing moving around here is a dirty guy pushing a shopping cart full of cans.

"We started a Facebook group and found out we have a lot more in common than previously suspected."

"Yeah, I managed you all. So what?" Irv dribbles the ball against his knee and it skips across the hot pavement.

"It's called a class action lawsuit. Your attorney should be getting the paperwork soon. We're hauling you in for mismanagement."

"I made you guys stars!" The thin hairs that normally run across Irv's scalp are wetted down and slouching over his forehead.

Gerardo's voice gets really loud: "You ruined our careers! Biz Markie deejays at a strip club now. Jesus Jones was deported back to England." Gerardo steps in close to Irv. I crawl on my hands and knees to catch all necessary

71

transcription. "I promised I wouldn't say anything," his voice is a hiss, hard to hear with that dirty guy's squeaky shopping cart wheel, "but Right Said Fred sells hotdogs at the zoo."

"Oh Jesus," Irv says, wiping his forehead with his sleeve. "I'll fight it." His long, pale finger jabs Gerardo in the heart.

"You DO NOT go from singing '*Rico Suave*' on MTV and banging Kennedy in the men's room…" Gerardo says, knocking Irv's hand away and poking my boss in the chest. "…to *this*." He points at a long scar on the side of his torso.

"God, Gerardo, what happened to you?" My boss makes the same face as that day I brought him a spoiled chicken salad sandwich, and he spent the afternoon in the bathroom.

"What do you think, Irv? I had to sell my kidney on the black market. When you left me high and dry, I had a $100-a-day doo-rag habit. Think I'm proud of it?"

"Whoa, whoa, okay. I don't think we should talk anymore without lawyers present. This is totally…" He looks at me and raises an eyebrow to make sure I'm paying attention. "Totally bogus. You guys don't have a case."

"Take it all in." I can't stop looking at the pink and purple zig-zag down his side. "It's your fault."

Irv picks up his sports coat and tie and marches over to me. My boss slips his cell phone in my hand as we walk away. "Speed dial number four," he mumbles into my ear. His voice is panicked. "It's the Budweiser Frogs. Make sure they're cool. If Gerardo gets his claws into them, I'm sunk."

THE MANY LIVES OF
JAMES BROWN'S CAPES

JAMES BROWN DIED at the age of 73 on Christmas Day, 2006. The Godfather of Soul left a legacy of hit records, sold-out concerts and gallons of sweat.

Brown also left a sizable debt.

A year-and-a-half after his funeral, the majority of his South Carolina mansion was auctioned off in New York to pay his creditors. Over three hundred personal items—from costumes, furniture, dinnerware and even his hair dryer—were available for bidding. Men and women filled the auction house that summer day and flicked their bidding paddles through the air for a piece of the famed entertainer's life.

Lot 72 *Sex Machine Belt* (Estimated sale: $2,000-$3000/ Actual sale: $4,750)

Mister Xang stepped into the restaurant with his head held proud. The dinner crowd was paying dearly for the honor of filling up on beef cheek gnocchi and endive pudding at New York City's hippest restaurant. Not a face lifted and not a conversation broke as the small man from China waited nervously for the maitre'd.

Xang kept his black suit jacket on. "The time is not right to unbutton," he thought. "Savor the moment." He smiled as a couple, who spoke English too fast for him to interpret, walked past. "It's yours. It's yours. You are victorious, and these moments are rare," he reminded himself. "You need to appreciate it." He snuffed his nose as a feeling of happiness rushed through his body like he hadn't felt since that day in 1976. "They'll get their show soon enough."

His plan seemed like a gift to this crowd. Just like James gave every night on stage.

Xang ached at the thought he would never see his idol singing in person. James Brown played for thousands upon thousands of audiences, but never in Xang's home province back in China. In fact, Western records like Brown's were illegal until just recently.

But now that Xang could buy *Live at the Apollo* down the street, his urge to listen to the Hardest Working Man in Show Business had flat-lined. That music didn't feel special anymore.

This belt, though, made him feel special. Possibly, he told the butterflies kicking violently at his abdomen, it was even better than seeing the Godfather in concert.

"Can I help you, sir?" A man with no hair and a white mustache looked down at Xang. It took him a moment to answer. Xang's English was fine, but he was self-conscious. He calculated even the smallest public whisper, never wanting to leave the wrong impression.

The maitre'd's question hit the shy Chinese man like a spotlight from the rafters. In Xang's mind, he'd walked out on a dark Apollo stage and the emcee announced *him* as the hardest working man in show business. He stepped to the center of the room and heard the clattering silverware pause and saw the buzzing wait staff halt. "Where do the Sex Machines sit?" he announced and flapped open his suit.

The belt buckle weighed as much as one of the restaurant's serving dishes. Oval-shaped and carved with sharp right angles, the buckle's rhinestones glimmered above the lipstick red paint filling its background. Lifting out from the metal, like hands grasping for attention, were the chrome words: SEX MACHINE.

When the bidding began, and it sparkled under the bright lights, Xang knew he couldn't return home without it. He'd never felt a love this storybook perfect, not even when he first met his wife.

74

Xang's audience, who paid $500 a plate for dinner, *not* a show, gulped in silence. A few snickered. But most just kept on eating and talking. Xang knew not everyone would *get* the belt buckle. But he thought it'd be fun to kick up some trouble in New York while he was there. He was considered a dangerous political misfit back home and felt a compulsive need to leave his stamp on Gotham City. A weighty sadness fell over his body as he learned, standing before an unamused group of diners, that making no impression is a far more lonely feeling than making a bad one.

The buckle's secret newness had worn off, just as James' records did once they were available to the public. When Xang acquired a bootleg copy of the *Sex Machine* album in 1976 and played it low, so no one would suspect he possessed an illegal item, those butterflies first became his friends.

Now the butterflies were gone. Out on the sidewalk, looking at his waist, the chrome letters didn't seem to shine as bright as they did under the auction house lights, or even from behind the dark curtain of his suit coat. He wondered if anything ever would again.

Lot 65 *Red "JB's" Suit* (Estimated sale: $3,000-$4,000/ Actual sale: $9,375)

Cops threw their pencils in the air when they got frustrated. By the time the officer started asking questions, Fourteenth Avenue was as full of snapped pencils and annoyed policemen as it was of pigeon shit. "Think back hard, lady. You've got to give me something better than *this*." He pointed to the police sketch artist, the one guy who hadn't thrown his writing utensil in disgust.

Summer in New York was sticky. It had that dumpster-in-an-oven smell the officer hated so much. He wished he were back behind his desk, especially when a nearby squad car's blue and red lights spun blindingly into his eyes.

"I'm telling you…" The woman's dark hair was pulled back tight. Whenever she couldn't find the right word, like that moment, she bit her lip and snapped her fingers wildly. "It was a little guy. I don't know. What are you, like six-one? The guy probably came to your chest. He was a black guy. Maybe in his mid-50s."

"Right, right, right," the cop stretched his arms, hoping the carpal tunnel stinging in his wrist would disappear. Hoping either an employee or customer would give a straight answer to this fiasco so he could make the kids' soccer game. "Continue."

"He seemed really jittery. Maybe like he'd never done this before. Does that help?"

"Of course, continue." The officer's throat stung nearly as much as his wrist, and it killed him waiting for the rookie to bring an herbal tea.

"Um…" The woman had been robbed at gunpoint, bomb-point, knifepoint and even blowtorch-point during her twenty-seven years at the bank. But never like this. After all those other robberies, panicky asthma always left her a nervous wreck. But today's robbery didn't. She thought that was funny. "He had big hair, like a-couple-hours-at-the-beauty-parlor big. An enormous black pompadour like brothers used to sport in the 60s—you know, lots of product—before afros came into style."

The officer slowed his breathing to erase all the non-bank robbery thoughts. "Yes, ma'am, I know. Jerry here, the sketch artist, he's shown me the picture."

"That's about all, sir. I mean, it sounds crazy, but the guy *looked* like James Brown. The singer, you know. 'I feel good' and all that."

"Ma'am, James Brown is dead. He didn't rob your bank. Let's go into the incident with a little more detail."

Someone knocked into the officer's back, running yellow tape across the street to mark off the crime scene.

The officer held the urge to tear that guy a new one.

"He was wearing this red polyester jumpsuit, the color of fake blood in the movies. It had rhinestones along all the seams. I'm talking head-to-toe. And a shiny lamè cape, the same color of red, with these sparklies along the collar. It had 'JB's' outlined in fake diamonds, too."

"That's a first, I have to admit." The cop gave up hope for soccer and looked at the sliver of blue sky above downtown's buildings. He got lost watching the bank's flag snap in the breeze overhead. "Alright, did he pull a weapon on you? I mean, how did you know you were being robbed?"

"Easy," the woman laughed and took another sip of coffee from a paper cup. "He passed me a note."

"Hey, that's great. *That's* helpful. Do you have it?" A burst of relief spread through the officer, making him forget about the stinging in his throat and wrist.

"I can't make heads or tails. Maybe you can." She passed a scrap of cardstock, which the forensics lab would later connect to a brochure from a popular auction house.

It read: "Give me $9, 375 or I'll be in deep shit with my wife."

Lot 136 *Cancelled Checks* (Estimated Sale: $1,500-$2,000/ Actual Sale: $1,500)

Fifteen years after the auction's gavel last slammed down, Jerome Bradley throws another birthday card in the trash of his Kansas City home.

He just mowed the yard and is covered in sweat. A salty drop from his forehead smacks right on the slip of paper he found in the card. He mumbles angrily under his breath as he looks for his wife.

Vivian doesn't turn around when he enters the bedroom. She just inhales deep. "Mmmmm," she says. "I love the smell of fresh cut grass. It's relaxing."

"I'm glad someone can relax around here," Jerome says, taking off his boots, spackled in yard clippings. "Your brother thinks he's really funny, doesn't he?"

"Still? How many of those do you think he has?" Vivian says, brushing her beautiful black hair in the vanity's mirror. "Just forget it and put on your suit. Your children are throwing you," she whispers now, "a surprise party in an hour. Don't forget."

"Honestly, Viv, your brother might be like one of those guys who seals all his toenail clippings in a plastic baggie. Catalogs them and stuff." He throws the cancelled check from the Mrs. James Brown Household across the makeup table. The check is dated from 1976, with a giant red "Paid" stamp across it. It was written for eighty-three dollars. "He's held onto this joke for fifteen years. He needs…"

Vivian puts the brush down as her voice jumps into an intimidating register. "Don't you dare say my brother needs a doctor again!" She burns a look through the birthday boy. Behind him, the wind blows the tree outside their window until a branch randomly taps the glass. "We go through this every year. Just forget it. You're fifty years old, Jerome. Act it."

"I'm just saying, he's got one of those obsessive personalities. And I don't want to be the thing he's obsessing about. I'll end up in one of those baggies someday."

"He thinks you think it's funny," she says, pulling out one dress after another from the closet and laying them across their tidy bed. "That's all."

"There's nothing funny about a grown man sending another grown man cancelled checks from James Brown on his birthday. I mentioned one time in 1995, *one time,* that I liked the guy's music."

"You've got to stop avoiding my brother. He's harmless." Vivian's eyes told Jerome her patience was about as tall as their grass now.

"Where does someone even *get* those old checks? I don't remember, but James Brown died naturally right? He wasn't murdered by an obsessive fan, was he? Because I could see that screwball sticking a knife in the Godfather of Soul and only stealing worthless scraps of shit like this."

She grinned into the mirror. "Well then, imagine what he'd steal after you."

Lot 239 *Military Style Suits* (Estimated Sale: $3,000-$5,000/ Actual Sale: $3,750)

"We have to be the faggiest looking army in history," Private Russell said, tugging on the ill-fitting uniform, wishing every step didn't make the buttons around his belly nearly fire off like a rocket launcher.

"Sergeant Pepper's is more like it," Private Adlaf grumbled, marching in formation through the hard dirt next to his three fellow soldiers and their leader. He struggled for air, never having trained this hard in his life.

"It's never too late to turn a negative into a positive, gentlemen," the Commander said. He repeated this mantra so often it came to the soldiers while they slept. Russell always wondered why the Commander's voice sounded strangely weak when repeating it, and for that matter, what the hell was he talking about?

If a visitor would have crawled through the thickets of forest and the army's ten foot razor wire fence that balmy Georgia day, they would have spied the world's most colorful five-man squadron.

Were they the Color Wheel Army? No, not exactly. But their uniforms were close. One blue, one green, one orange and one black for the infantrymen—all bold enough to be candy bar wrappers.

Their Commander wore a stunning merlot purple suit with a "JB" patch on the heart. Each had nifty white piping around the shoulders, collar and cuffs, all accentuated by the large brass buttons down the front.

Were they some sort of Rainbow Coalition? Not in the slightest. In fact, any mention of that idea would have met the asker with a fist in the mouth.

They were white supremacists, and proud of it. *"Were,"* being the key word. The ragtag, unnamed malitia didn't know it yet, but its purple-clad leader had a plan.

The Commander noticed the soldiers were special somewhere around the time Private Severe ran through their mock mine field. "My god," he said, chomping on the pungent butt of a cigar, using a pair of binoculars to watch the man dodge imaginary explosives. "Have you ever seen another human with so much grace? It's like a ballet."

"A ballet that'll blow off your foot," Private Forward snarled. "What does that have to do with our mission?"

The Commander patted him on the back and fought the urge to tell Forward: "it's okay" or "you're just grumpy because of the heat" or "there are juice boxes in the cooler if you need one." Instead, the man-in-charge held in the caring, thoughtful urges that came so naturally. The Commander used to express himself on a daily basis, but recently started bottling up his emotions. "Your mission to kill African Americans depends heavily on *gracefulness*, Private."

The muscular, edgy soldier jumped in before the Commander was through. "You mean the *blacks*? Don't get me started about how they took all the good basketball jobs. You think Pistol Pete Maravich could get a spot on any bench in America today? Not to mention how their *Latino* brothers are filling all the positions in baseball." The man lobbed a tobacco spit into the dry red dirt. "All these immigrants stealing things. Shit, no wonder this country's unemployment is so bad."

The Commander looked down at their drab green canvas uniforms and frowned. Their clothes were just as faded and horrifying as Private Forward' views on race relations.

80

The Commander fought another urge to explain that most of those people were actually citizens and that maybe the private should direct his anger into something more positive, like dancing. Had he ever watched *Footloose?*

But no, the Commander kept those things locked up tight, too. He didn't want to blow his last chance to turn a negative into a positive.

Later in their training, the Commander vowed never to keep his mouth shut again after watching Private Adlaf's raw strength and power in hand-to-hand combat drills. Coordination like that would take years of practice at Julliard.

"All right," the Commander said through his cigar, turning around and admiring his squad's colorful uniforms, reminding himself to have them sent to the dry cleaner before Tuesday. "Good run, men. I've done some research and I've cracked the code. If we want to destroy the enemy, there's one surefire way."

"Pipebombs?" Russell said with arched eyebrows.

"Poison their drinking water?" Adlaf shouted with confident, deranged eyes.

"Castration?" Severe popped his knuckles like a pro wrestler.

The Commander's cigar dropped to the ground with a red dust puff. His concrete face was frozen in a disgusted twist, like he just witnessed a dog relieving itself on the Bolshoi Ballet's stage. "No, son," he said fatherly, marching silently for a moment, watching his beautifully purple legs scissor back and forth, satisfied they had made the switch from those olive green fatigues. "It's the dawn of a new era for, uh, you white supremacists. It started months ago when I noticed a spark in your eyes." The Commander looked at each man's tender, hopeful face. "The best I've ever seen, and I've trained some of the finest squadrons of Neo-Nazis on the planet. You all know that; that's why you hired me."

The Commander hadn't, actually. He spent fourteen

81

years working in New York in a much more peaceful industry than racism and paramilitary operations. But times were tough, and he couldn't make ends meet in his former line of work, so the Commander fudged his resume—just a touch—and landed this gig down in Georgia.

"Now don't be angry, but last week when you sent me north to purchase that shoulder fired surface-to-air rocket launcher, I took a little detour. I couldn't help myself when I thought about the way you men stabbed those mannequins with your bayonets, all in sync, and in 4/4 time, no less," his voice grew airy, almost like a dream's voiceover, "like the Sharks in *West Side Story.*"

The soldiers' reactions—tense fists, toothy sneers and one flicking some nose goop at their leader—told him they weren't ready for the truth. The Commander decided to drop them into the pool gently. He sighed and reminded himself to substitute "Blood-Thirsty Commando Unit" for "All-Star Dance Troupe" when he made speeches.

"Well, I didn't buy that rocket launcher. Instead, I purchased these uniforms. Which," his voice leaped, cutting off the grumbling and near-revolt happening in their small ranks, "is the first step toward annihilating, you know, eh, an...entire...race...of people, or whatever."

He downplayed the racism card as much as possible. It made his shoulders tense and his neck hurt just thinking about the army's mission statement. It actually gave him violet stomach cramps.

The Commander nearly walked away from the army two weeks ago, but his world came together during a simulated siege of the NAACP offices. The men moved swiftly and effortlessly together. Their feet didn't tangle. They didn't speak, but knew what the others were thinking. It reminded the Commander of the best dancers he'd ever coached on Broadway.

Oh, god, he missed the bright lights and the quiet crowd chatter before shows. He thought he'd never get them back, but then Private Adlaf lifted Russell by the waist and spun him through the air. It was intended to quickly decapitate the mannequin representing the NAACP President, but the Commander saw pure, unfiltered dance magic.

"It's never too late to turn a negative into a positive," the Commander whispered to himself at the sight of Russell's twirling. He didn't so much lose his job as he was forced to leave the choreographer's chair, and the prospect of fixing the disaster he left in the Big Apple with this rag-tag bunch of southern boys filled him with excitement. That evening their smoke-filled underground training facility found a beam of sunshine when their leader realized that—with the right costumes, the right training and some snappy jazz fusion tunes—these guys could be bigger than Riverdance.

The Commander spat into the ground. It felt good to have that cigar out. It tasted icky and he had to brush his teeth about ten times a night before the flavor would pull itself from his taste buds. "Now stick with me here, men, but we're going to try some new footwork drills."

He clicked on the booming public address system.

"What is that?" one said, looking up at the enormous speakers.

"It's the theme from *Cats*, now trust me here. Unless you want to lose and not kill, you know, black people. I mean, I trained a whole Serbian death squad to *Cats*. But if you guys don't want to be the best…" the Commander turned his back to the group.

"Now, fellas. Fall in line, listen to your commander," Adlaf said, swaying his hips to the beat.

The Commander always knew Adlaf was a natural.

"Do you want to be the best?" the Commander yelled, picturing these four strutting and sliding across a New York stage before hot lights and breathless audiences.

"Yes, sir!" they all shouted and began taping their feet.

JOHNNY APPLESEED'S PUNCHATERIA

HIYA, PUT 'ER THERE! I'm Johnny Appleseed.

Wow, that's some grip! We could use a guy like you around here.

I bet you're asking yourself, "whoa, what the hell did I just step into? I was enjoying a leisurely visit to Danbury, Connecticut's finest mall. Me, my wife and our two little girls were just looking for the hot pretzel stand. I swear to god it used to be between the Suncoast Videos and that store that sells crappy-looking African do-dads. But *this*, this ain't like no pretzel store I ever seen."

And you'd be right for thinking that. Auntie Annie's moved downstairs across from the arcade, incidentally.

And I bet you're thinking to yourself, "whoa! Now this *guy* with an apple for a head and some enormous freaking muscles is squeezing my paw." I bet you're also thinking, "who is this collection of roughnecks and freaks behind him?"

Slow down, trigger. We'll get to my associates. But first let me ask a question: You got a boss?

Yeah, I thought so. Everybody answers to someone. And I bet he's a real prick.

Oh, she?

I bet *she*'s a real prick sometimes. Are you ever sitting in a meeting, all antsy and bored to death, wishing…no, *praying* that the next time Johnson from accounting stands up to read the numbers, maybe he'll walk on over and sock Madame Ball-Buster right in the neck?

No?

Really?

You just pulling my leg because these impressionable children of yours are running around?

Still no, eh? Well, you ever hoped somebody'd deliver the boss a middleweight-style punch in the kidneys?

Ah ha! That's what I'm talking about! As soon as you and your lovely family walked in, probably straight from Easter mass, judging by that tie you're wearing, I said to myself, "Him, that's a kidney man, through and through." I get it, brother. You're a sensible son-of-a-bitch. Kudos.

Well, let me say... Pardon me. I didn't get your name.

Frank, let me say that you've come to the right place. I'm Johnny Appleseed, and this is my store, the Punchateria.

Chances are, Frank, you've seen an operation like this before.

No?

Well, let me tell you how it works. I'm sure you noticed these little booths lining the walls, and within each of those booths is a pretty beefy dude or a butch chick. I see your wife has taken a shine to Javier. He's a great choice, but a little soft on the kidney punches.

See, the Punchateria knows about that built up rage inside us. But things ain't like they used to be. I'm talking about back when our dads could settle a disagreement about how many toes the Queen of England had with a fistfight. Geez, nowadays, you'd end up with a lawsuit, you do something as innocent as slap a waitress.

This was the problem I encountered a few years back. See, I hated this cocksucker...sorry girls, cover your ears. This *cocksucker* my ex-wife was dating. I wanted this jerk to wear my tire iron as a hat, you know? But you can't just go around whoopin' on every dude nailing Mrs. Appleseed in this day and age. I'd lose my visitation rights with the little Appleseeds, plus he'd probably sue me for every penny I got. So, I give my buddy, Doyle, thirty bucks to clock this homewrecker a few times on the lips.

Sure enough, when I pick my kids up that Friday, numbnuts has two black eyes and a missing tooth. One of the front ones you eat corn with. You know, the good teeth.

So, I figure I can't be the only fella on the planet with these problems.

...oh, no, no, no honey. Sir, I wouldn't let your little girl get too close to Snake. He used to work at Toys 'R' Us, and let's just say he's not against jabbing some toddler eyeballs. Good worker though, always on time, and one *hell* of a puncher. Seventy-eight inch reach. Once clocked a nun from across the street.

Where was I, Frank? Right, so I opened this place up, Johnny Appleseed's Punchateria. Like the name implies, you walk through, cafeteria-style, talk to my employees and decide which one you'd like to have punch someone for you. It's a flat rate for a single sock in the face. However, added brutality can be tacked on for a nominal fee. Kind of like getting a little box of chicken nuggets with your meal at Wendy's.

Say your parole officer has been really jamming you in the ass lately. Felix over here will clobber that dude, no sweat. You never get your hands dirty, but have all the satisfaction of punching 'em yourself. You got a P.O.? We do phenomenal work on parole officers. They're probably our number one target.

Or let's say your brother-in-law, that bastard who always makes you look dumb in front of your wife. Let's say he has a birthday coming up. For a few pennies more, Constantine—how could you miss Constantine; he was a wrestler at Yale until he fell on hard times—will dress like a clown and *actually* sing Happy Birthday at this guy's door. We could even time it so you're over there for his birthday party, watching his face glow all warm and rosy with this touching surprise. Have that bastard get all, "who did this? You guys are the greatest!" Meanwhile, Constantine finishes the song and says, "surprise, you've got a broken nose!" And BAM! Your brother-in-law falls to the floor. Blood is spurtin' everywhere, and he's crying like some wounded animal. Nobody knows you were to blame. Doesn't that sound sweet?

Rage is a tricky business, Mister...ah?

86

Rosengarten, Frank Rosengarten. That's a good name. Huh. Oh, sorry, I spaced out. Your name sounds familiar.

Look, bro, I see your wife and Javier are getting along real nice. And she's out of earshot, so I'll talk to you straight. This place ain't just a one-way street, if you catch me. I can tell you're a little like me. Sometimes we just need some attention for ourselves. You know what I'm saying… sometimes a man has a sickness of the soul. An emotional pit that only a punch in the face can fix. Yeah, now you're catching on. You can request us to punch *you*. Now we don't get into any of that kinky sex shit; that's your business. But sometimes a man needs to get himself socked to align his chakras and all that mumbo jumbo. That's all I'm saying. We'll leave it at that.

Anyhow, that's what we do at the Punchateria. Take a look around the showroom floor, ask the guys questions, just don't get your fingers near their mouths. If you are interested in our services, all we need is a major credit card, the victim's name and a time you'd like the job done. And let me assure you, we will try our hardest not to kill anyone.

Well, let me be honest. Yes, we did lose one person. But Rodney said that guy was *old*. Like on a feeding tube or something. Said he hardly karate chopped the guy's throat before that heart monitor thingy went dead. I'd say that was an act of god.

Also, your name is kept strictly confidential. We will not reveal your identity unless you'd like us to say something classy like: "How's that taste, Burt Reynolds? Maybe next time you'll spend the extra few seconds to give Judy Mayflower that autograph when you run into her outside of Chili's." But that, too, costs extra.

Frank Rosengarten, my friend, you will be hooked. Let me tell you. Clients claim their blood pressure and stress levels have never been lower. Think of it, you have the freedom to bust anyone in the chops. Might I add that Tanya over there in the corner is a month behind on her boat payment, so now she's having a buy-one-get-one-free sale. You won't find a cheaper punch in the face at the Danbury Mall.

Excuse me, something just occurred to me. I need to check my daily planner.

* * *

You're Frank Rosengarten? The same Frank Rosengarten who lives on Savannah Drive and works at Regal Auto Detailing?

Oh boy.

You're Frank *Richard* Rosengarten?

Damn.

I hate to do this, kid. Close your eyes.

* * *

Frank, hey. Wake up, buddy. Wake up. Sorry I punched you in the face like that. I took it as easy as possible. Um, see, that was from your boss, Shirley Jacobs. She wanted me to tell you, quote, "Frank, you bastard. How dare you think of having me punched? I knew I couldn't trust you. You're fired."

Tough break, kid.

You want I should punch her back? Only fifty bucks.

(Photo by Leah Wensink)

ABOUT THE AUTHOR

Patrick Wensink does not live in a sex dungeon.
He lives in Louisville, KY with this wife (who also
doesn't live in a sex dungeon, thank you very much).
His short stories appear in Hobart and Monkeybicycle.
He even had a greeting card published once. He is
currently working on his first novel.

Learn about all things Wentastic at:
www.patrickwensink.com

Bizarro books

CATALOG   SPRING 2009

Bizarro Books publishes under the following imprints:

www.rawdogscreamingpress.com

www.eraserheadpress.com

www.afterbirthbooks.com

www.swallowdownpress.com

For all your Bizarro needs visit:

WWW.BIZARROCENTRAL.COM

Introduce yourselves to the bizarro genre and all of its authors with the Bizarro Starter Kit series. Each volume features short novels and short stories by ten of the leading bizarro authors, designed to give you a perfect sampling of the genre for only $5 plus shipping.

BB-0X1
"The Bizarro Starter Kit" (Orange)

Featuring D. Harlan Wilson, Carlton Mellick III, Jeremy Robert Johnson, Kevin L Donihe, Gina Ranalli, Andre Duza, Vincent W. Sakowski, Steve Beard, John Edward Lawson, and Bruce Taylor.

236 pages $5

BB-0X2
"The Bizarro Starter Kit" (Blue)

Featuring Ray Fracalossy, Jeremy C. Shipp, Jordan Krall, Mykle Hansen, Andersen Prunty, Eckhard Gerdes, Bradley Sands, Steve Aylett, Christian TeBordo, and Tony Rauch.

244 pages $5

BB-001 "The Kafka Effekt" D. Harlan Wilson - A collection of forty-four irreal short stories loosely written in the vein of Franz Kafka, with more than a pinch of William S. Burroughs sprinkled on top. **211 pages $14**

BB-002 "Satan Burger" Carlton Mellick III - The cult novel that put Carlton Mellick III on the map ... Six punks get jobs at a fast food restaurant owned by the devil in a city violently overpopulated by surreal alien cultures. **236 pages $14**

BB-003 "Some Things Are Better Left Unplugged" Vincent Sakwoski - Join The Man and his Nemesis, the obese tabby, for a nightmare roller coaster ride into this postmodern fantasy. **152 pages $10**

BB-004 "Shall We Gather At the Garden?" Kevin L Donihe - Donihe's Debut novel. Midgets take over the world, The Church of Lionel Richie vs. The Church of the Byrds, plant porn and more! **244 pages $14**

BB-005 "Razor Wire Pubic Hair" Carlton Mellick III - A genderless humandildo is purchased by a razor dominatrix and brought into her nightmarish world of bizarre sex and mutilation. **176 pages $11**

BB-006 "Stranger on the Loose" D. Harlan Wilson - The fiction of Wilson's 2nd collection is planted in the soil of normalcy, but what grows out of that soil is a dark, witty, otherworldly jungle... **228 pages $14**

BB-007 "The Baby Jesus Butt Plug" Carlton Mellick III - Using clones of the Baby Jesus for anal sex will be the hip sex fetish of the future. **92 pages $10**

BB-008 "Fishyfleshed" Carlton Mellick III - The world of the past is an illogical flatland lacking in dimension and color, a sick-scape of crispy squid people wandering the desert for no apparent reason. **260 pages $14**

BB-009 **"Dead Bitch Army" Andre Duza** - Step into a world filled with racist teenagers, cannibals, 100 warped Uncle Sams, automobiles with razor-sharp teeth, living graffiti, and a pissed-off zombie bitch out for revenge. **344 pages $16**

BB-010 **"The Menstruating Mall" Carlton Mellick III** - "The Breakfast Club meets Chopping Mall as directed by David Lynch." - Brian Keene **212 pages $12**

BB-011 **"Angel Dust Apocalypse" Jeremy Robert Johnson** - Meth-heads, man-made monsters, and murderous Neo-Nazis. "Seriously amazing short stories..." - Chuck Palahniuk, author of Fight Club **184 pages $11**

BB-012 **"Ocean of Lard" Kevin L Donihe / Carlton Mellick III** - A parody of those old Choose Your Own Adventure kid's books about some very odd pirates sailing on a sea made of animal fat. **176 pages $12**

BB-013 **"Last Burn in Hell" John Edward Lawson** - From his lurid angst-affair with a lesbian music diva to his ascendance as unlikely pop icon the one constant for Kenrick Brimley, official state prison gigolo, is he's got no clue what he's doing. **172 pages $14**

BB-014 **"Tangerinephant" Kevin Dole 2** - TV-obsessed aliens have abducted Michael Tangerinephant in this bizarro combination of science fiction, satire, and surrealism. **164 pages $11**

BB-015 **"Foop!" Chris Genoa** - Strange happenings are going on at Dactyl, Inc, the world's first and only time travel tourism company.

"A surreal pie in the face!" - Christopher Moore **300 pages $14**

BB-016 **"Spider Pie" Alyssa Sturgill** - A one-way trip down a rabbit hole inhabited by sexual deviants and friendly monsters, fairytale beginnings and hideous endings. **104 pages $11**

BB-017 "The Unauthorized Woman" Efrem Emerson - Enter the world of the inner freak, a landscape populated by the pre-dead and morticioners, by cockroaches and 300-lb robots. **104 pages $11**

BB-018 "Fugue XXIX" Forrest Aguirre - Tales from the fringe of speculative literary fiction where innovative minds dream up the future's uncharted territories while mining forgotten treasures of the past. **220 pages $16**

BB-019 "Pocket Full of Loose Razorblades" John Edward Lawson - A collection of dark bizarro stories. From a giant rectum to a foot-fungus factory to a girl with a biforked tongue. **190 pages $13**

BB-020 "Punk Land" Carlton Mellick III - In the punk version of Heaven, the anarchist utopia is threatened by corporate fascism and only Goblin, Mortician's sperm, and a blue-mohawked female assassin named Shark Girl can stop them. **284 pages $15**

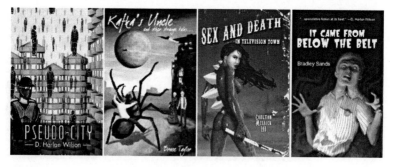

BB-021 "Pseudo-City" D. Harlan Wilson - Pseudo-City exposes what waits in the bathroom stall, under the manhole cover and in the corporate boardroom, all in a way that can only be described as mind-bogglingly irreal. **220 pages $16**

BB-022 "Kafka's Uncle and Other Strange Tales" Bruce Taylor - Anslenot and his giant tarantula (tormentor? fri-end?) wander a desecrated world in this novel and collection of stories from Mr. Magic Realism Himself. **348 pages $17**

BB-023 "Sex and Death In Television Town" Carlton Mellick III - In the old west, a gang of hermaphrodite gunslingers take refuge from a demon plague in Telos: a town where its citizens have televisions instead of heads. **184 pages $12**

BB-024 "It Came From Below The Belt" Bradley Sands - What can Grover Goldstein do when his severed, sentient penis forces him to return to high school and help it win the presidential election? **204 pages $13**

BB-025 **"Sick: An Anthology of Illness" John Lawson, editor** - These Sick stories are horrendous and hilarious dissections of creative minds on the scalpel's edge. **296 pages $16**

BB-026 **"Tempting Disaster" John Lawson, editor** - A shocking and alluring anthology from the fringe that examines our culture's obsession with taboos. **260 pages $16**

BB-027 **"Siren Promised" Jeremy Robert Johnson** - Nominated for the Bram Stoker Award. A potent mix of bad drugs, bad dreams, brutal bad guys, and surreal/ incredible art by Alan M. Clark. **190 pages $13**

BB-028 **"Chemical Gardens" Gina Ranalli** - Ro and punk band Green is the Enemy find Kreepkins, a surfer-dude warlock, a vengeful demon, and a Metal Priestess in their way as they try to escape an underground nightmare. **188 pages $13**

BB-029 **"Jesus Freaks" Andre Duza** - For God so loved the world that he gave his only two begotten sons… and a few million zombies. **400 pages $16**

BB-030 **"Grape City" Kevin L. Donihe** - More Donihe-style comedic bizarro about a demon named Charles who is forced to work a minimum wage job on Earth after Hell goes out of business. **108 pages $10**

BB-031 **"Sea of the Patchwork Cats" Carlton Mellick III** - A quiet dreamlike tale set in the ashes of the human race. For Mellick enthusiasts who also adore The Twilight Zone. **112 pages $10**

BB-032 **"Extinction Journals" Jeremy Robert Johnson** - An uncanny voyage across a newly nuclear America where one man must confront the problems associated with loneliness, insane dieties, radiation, love, and an ever-evolving cockroach suit with a mind of its own. **104 pages $10**

BB-033 **"Meat Puppet Cabaret" Steve Beard** - At last! The secret connection between Jack the Ripper and Princess Diana's death revealed! **240 pages $16 / $30**

BB-034 **"The Greatest Fucking Moment in Sports" Kevin L. Donihe** - In the tradition of the surreal anti-sitcom Get A Life comes a tale of triumph and agape love from the master of comedic bizarro. **108 pages $10**

BB-035 **"The Troublesome Amputee" John Edward Lawson** - Disturbing verse from a man who truly believes nothing is sacred and intends to prove it. **104 pages $9**

BB-036 **"Deity" Vic Mudd** - God (who doesn't like to be called "God") comes down to a typical, suburban, Ohio family for a little vacation—but it doesn't turn out to be as relaxing as He had hoped it would be... **168 pages $12**

BB-037 **"The Haunted Vagina" Carlton Mellick III** - It's difficult to love a woman whose vagina is a gateway to the world of the dead. **132 pages $10**

BB-038 **"Tales from the Vinegar Wasteland" Ray Fracalossy** - Witness: a man is slowly losing his face, a neighbor who periodically screams out for no apparent reason, and a house with a room that doesn't actually exist. **240 pages $14**

BB-039 **"Suicide Girls in the Afterlife" Gina Ranalli** - After Pogue commits suicide, she unexpectedly finds herself an unwilling "guest" at a hotel in the Afterlife, where she meets a group of bizarre characters, including a goth Satan, a hippie Jesus, and an alien-human hybrid. **100 pages $9**

BB-040 **"And Your Point Is?" Steve Aylett** - In this follow-up to LINT multiple authors provide critical commentary and essays about Jeff Lint's mind-bending literature. **104 pages $11**

BB-041 **"Not Quite One of the Boys" Vincent Sakowski** - While drug-dealer Maxi drinks with Dante in purgatory, God and Satan play a little tri-level chess and do a little bargaining over his business partner, Vinnie, who is still left on earth. **220 pages $14**

BB-042 **"Teeth and Tongue Landscape" Carlton Mellick III** - On a planet made out of meat, a socially-obsessive monophobic man tries to find his place amongst the strange creatures and communities that he comes across. **110 pages $10**

BB-043 **"War Slut" Carlton Mellick III** - Part "1984," part "Waiting for Godot," and part action horror video game adaptation of John Carpenter's "The Thing." **116 pages $10**

BB-044 **"All Encompassing Trip" Nicole Del Sesto** - In a world where coffee is no longer available, the only television shows are reality TV re-runs, and the animals are talking back, Nikki, Amber and a singing Coyote in a do-rag are out to restore the light **308 pages $15**

BB-045 **"Dr. Identity" D. Harlan Wilson** - Follow the Dystopian Duo on a killing spree of epic proportions through the irreal postcapitalist city of Bliptown where time ticks sideways, artificial Bug-Eyed Monsters punish citizens for consumer-capitalist lethargy, and ultraviolence is as essential as a daily multivitamin. **208 pages $15**

BB-046 **"The Million-Year Centipede" Eckhard Gerdes** - Wakelin, frontman for 'The Hinge,' wrote a poem so prophetic that to ignore it dooms a person to drown in blood. **130 pages $12**

BB-047 **"Sausagey Santa" Carlton Mellick III** - A bizarro Christmas tale featuring Santa as a piratey mutant with a body made of sausages. 124 pages $10

BB-048 **"Misadventures in a Thumbnail Universe" Vincent Sakowski** - Dive deep into the surreal and satirical realms of neo-classical Blender Fiction, filled with television shoes and flesh-filled skies. **120 pages $10**

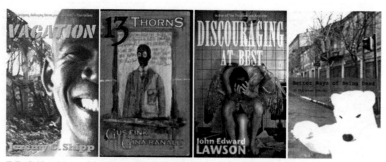

BB-049 **"Vacation" Jeremy C. Shipp** - Blueblood Bernard Johnson leaving his boring life behind to go on The Vacation, a year-long corporate sponsored odyssey. But instead of seeing the world, Bernard is captured by terrorists, becomes a key figure in secret drug wars, and, worse, doesn't once miss his secure American Dream. **160 pages $14**

BB-051 **"13 Thorns" Gina Ranalli** - Thirteen tales of twisted, bizarro horror. **240 pages $13**

BB-050 **"Discouraging at Best" John Edward Lawson** - A collection where the absurdity of the mundane expands exponentially creating a tidal wave that sweeps reason away. For those who enjoy satire, bizarro, or a good old-fashioned slap to the senses. **208 pages $15**

BB-052 **"Better Ways of Being Dead" Christian TeBordo** - In this class, the students have to keep one palm down on the table at all times, and listen to lectures about a panda who speaks Chinese. **216 pages $14**

BB-053 **"Ballad of a Slow Poisoner" Andrew Goldfarb** Millford Mutterwurst sat down on a Tuesday to take his afternoon tea, and made the unpleasant discovery that his elbows were becoming flatter. **128 pages $10**

BB-054 **"Wall of Kiss" Gina Ranalli** - A woman... A wall... Sometimes love blooms in the strangest of places. **108 pages $9**

BB-055 **"HELP! A Bear is Eating Me" Mykle Hansen** - The bizarro, heartwarming, magical tale of poor planning, hubris and severe blood loss... **150 pages $11**

BB-056 **"Piecemeal June" Jordan Krall** - A man falls in love with a living sex doll, but with love comes danger when her creator comes after her with crab-squid assassins. **90 pages $9**

BB-057 **"Laredo" Tony Rauch** - Dreamlike, surreal stories by Tony Rauch. **180 pages $12**

BB-058 **"The Overwhelming Urge" Andersen Prunty** - A collection of bizarro tales by Andersen Prunty. **150 pages $11**

BB-059 **"Adolf in Wonderland" Carlton Mellick III** - A dreamlike adventure that takes a young descendant of Adolf Hitler's design and sends him down the rabbit hole into a world of imperfection and disorder. **180 pages $11**

BB-060 **"Super Cell Anemia" Duncan B. Barlow** - "Unrelentingly bizarre and mysterious, unsettling in all the right ways..." - Brian Evenson. **180 pages $12**

BB-061 **"Ultra Fuckers" Carlton Mellick III** - Absurdist suburban horror about a couple who enter an upper middle class gated community but can't find their way out. **108 pages $9**

BB-062 **"House of Houses" Kevin L. Donihe** - An odd man wants to marry his house. Unfortunately, all of the houses in the world collapse at the same time in the Great House Holocaust. Now he must travel to House Heaven to find his departed fiancee. **172 pages $11**

BB-063 **"Necro Sex Machine" Andre Duza** - The Dead Bicth returns in this follow-up to the bizarro zombie epic Dead Bitch Army. **400 pages $16**

BB-064 **"Squid Pulp Blues" Jordan Krall** - In these three bizarro-noir novellas, the reader is thrown into a world of murderers, drugs made from squid parts, deformed gun-toting veterans, and a mischievous apocalyptic donkey. **204 pages $12**

BB-065 **"Jack and Mr. Grin" Andersen Prunty** - "When Mr. Grin calls you can hear a smile in his voice. Not a warm and friendly smile, but the kind that seizes your spine in fear. You don't need to pay your phone bill to hear it. That smile is in every line of Prunty's prose." - Tom Bradley. **208 pages $12**

BB-066 **"Cybernetrix" Carlton Mellick III** - What would you do if your normal everyday world was slowly mutating into the video game world from Tron? **212 pages $12**

BB-067 **"Lemur" Tom Bradley** - Spencer Sproul is a would-be serial-killing bus boy who can't manage to murder, injure, or even scare anybody. However, there are other ways to do damage to far more people and do it legally... **120 pages $12**

BB-068 **"Cocoon of Terror" Jason Earls** - Decapitated corpses...a sculpture of terror...Zelian's masterpiece, his Cocoon of Terror, will trigger a supernatural disaster for everyone on Earth. **196 pages $14**

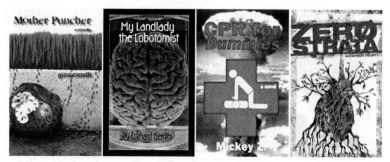

BB-069 **"Mother Puncher" Gina Ranalli** - The world has become tragically over-populated and now the government strongly opposes procreation. Ed is employed by the government as a mother-puncher. He doesn't relish his job, but he knows it has to be done and he knows he's the best one to do it. **120 pages $9**

BB-070 **"My Landlady the Lobotomist" Eckhard Gerdes** - The brains of past tenants line the shelves of my boarding house, soaking in a mysterious elixir. One more slip-up and the landlady might just add my frontal lobe to her collection. **116 pages $12**

BB-071 **"CPR for Dummies" Mickey Z.** - This hilarious freakshow at the world's end is the fragmented, sobering debut novel by acclaimed nonfiction author Mickey Z. **216 pages $14**

BB-072 **"Zerostrata" Andersen Prunty** - Hansel Nothing lives in a tree house, suffers from memory loss, has a very eccentric family, and falls in love with a woman who runs naked through the woods every night. **144 pages $11**

BB-073 "The Egg Man" Carlton Mellick III - It is a world where humans reproduce like insects. Children are the property of corporations, and having an enormous ten-foot brain implanted into your skull is a grotesque sexual fetish. Mellick's industrial urban dystopia is one of his darkest and grittiest to date. **184 pages $11**

BB-074 "Shark Hunting in Paradise Garden" Cameron Pierce - A group of strange humanoid religious fanatics travel back in time to the Garden of Eden to discover it is invested with hundreds of giant flying maneating sharks. **150 pages $10**

BB-075 "Apeshit" Carlton Mellick III - Friday the 13th meets Visitor Q. Six hipster teens go to a cabin in the woods inhabited by a deformed killer. An incredibly fucked-up parody of B-horror movies with a bizarro slant. **192 pages $12**

BB-076 "Rampaging Fuckers of Everything on the Crazy Shitting Planet of the Vomit At smosphere" Mykle Hansen - 3 bizarro satires. Monster Cocks, Journey to the Center of Agnes Cuddlebottom, and Crazy Shitting Planet. **228 pages $12**

BB-077 "The Kissing Bug" Daniel Scott Buck - In the tradition of Roald Dahl, Tim Burton, and Edward Gorey, comes this bizarro anti-war children's story about a bohemian conenose kissing bug who falls in love with a human woman. **116 pages $10**

BB-078 "MachoPoni" Lotus Rose - It's My Little Pony... *Bizarro* style! A long time ago Poniworld was split in two. On one side of the Jagged Line is the Pastel Kingdom, a magical land of music, parties, and positivity. On the other side of the Jagged Line is Dark Kingdom inhabited by an army of undead ponies. **148 pages $11**

BB-079 "The Faggiest Vampire" Carlton Mellick III - A Roald Dahl-esque children's story about two faggy vampires who partake in a mustache competition to find out which one is truly the faggiest. **104 pages $10**

BB-080 "Sky Tongues" Gina Ranalli - The autobiography of Sky Tongues, the biracial hermaphrodite actress with tongues for fingers. Follow her strange life story as she rises from freak to fame. **204 pages $12**

BB-081 **"Washer Mouth" Kevin L. Donihe** - A washing machine becomes human and pursues his dream of meeting his favorite soap opera star. **244 pages $11**

BB-082 **"Shatnerquake" Jeff Burk** - All of the characters ever played by William Shatner are suddenly sucked into our world. Their mission: hunt down and destroy the real William Shatner. **100 pages $10**

BB-083 **"The Cannibals of Candyland" Carlton Mellick III** - There exists a race of cannibals that are made of candy. They live in an underground world made out of candy. One man has dedicated his life to killing them all. **170 pages $11**

BB-084 **"Slub Glub in the Weird World of the Weeping Willows"** **Andrew Goldfarb** - The charming tale of a blue glob named Slub Glub who helps the weeping willows whose tears are flooding the earth. There are also hyenas, ghosts, and a voodoo priest **100 pages $10**

COMING SOON

"Fistful of Feet" by Jordan Krall
"Ass Goblins of Auschwitz" by Cameron Pierce
"Cursed" by Jeremy C. Shipp
"Warrior Wolf Women of the Wasteland"
by Carlton Mellick III
"The Kobold Wizard's Dildo of Enlightenment +2"
by Carlton Mellick III

ORDER FORM

TITLES	QTY	PRICE	TOTAL

Please make checks and moneyorders payable to ROSE O'KEEFE / BIZARRO BOOKS in U.S. funds only. Please don't send bad checks! Allow 2-6 weeks for delivery. International orders may take longer. If you'd like to pay online via PAYPAL.COM, send payments to publisher@eraserheadpress.com.

SHIPPING: US ORDERS - $2 for the first book, $1 for each additional book. For priority shipping, add an additional $4. INT'L ORDERS - $5 for the first book, $3 for each additional book. Add an additional $5 per book for global priority shipping.

Send payment to:

BIZARRO BOOKS
  C/O Rose O'Keefe
  205 NE Bryant
  Portland, OR 97211

Address

City   State   Zip

Email   Phone

Lightning Source UK Ltd.
Milton Keynes UK
23 November 2009

146624UK00001B/60/P